Long Shadows

When Jake Rudd is saved from a brutal beating, he can't believe his luck. Not only is his saviour an attractive redhead, she's an old flame. Suddenly his plans to settle down seem a real possibility. Unfortunately, Ros West has no memory of him, and with trouble following her, no reason to trust him. Only when family and friends are threatened by a power-hungry businessman, do the long shadows of the past bring events full circle.

Now, side by side, Jake and Ros must deal with the past to secure the future. But when the smoke clears, will old scores be settled or will the truth prove more dangerous than a smoking gun?

Long Shadows

Terry James

A Black Horse Western

ROBERT HALE · LONDON

ISBN 978-0-7090-8740-3

Robert Hale Limited
Clerkenwell House
Clerkenwell Green
London EC1R 0HT

www.halebooks.com

Typeset by
Derek Doyle & Associates, Shaw Heath
Printed and bound in Great Britain by
CPI Antony Rowe, Chippenham and Eastbourne

CHAPTER 1

'You know the horse is worth that much without the saddle.' Fighting her indignation, Ros West frowned at the forty dollars sitting in the hostler's calloused palm. 'Are you sure that's the best you can do?'

The wrinkled livery owner looked her over from the toes of her muddy boots to the top of her felt hat then spat a stream of tobacco. 'Lady, times are hard. Take it or leave it. Either way, I won't lose any sleep.'

'I bet you won't,' she grumbled, snatching the money and fumbling it into her saddle-bags.

Without another glance at the wily old trader, she slung the bags across her shoulder and left the livery with a dry throat and a short temper. It had been a long day and she hadn't wanted to arrive in town after dark. The shadows might hold too many surprises, and right now, she could do without any more problems.

'Damn horse,' she mumbled, limping to ease the ache in her feet.

The animal had thrown a shoe and she'd had to walk the last three miles through pouring rain over rough terrain. Not only was she wet through to the skin, her boots had rubbed blisters on her heels.

She struggled to keep her irritation in check and sidestepped a drunk before stumbling off the board-walk. Besides her cussing, the distinct grunts and thuds of someone being beaten scorched the air. She increased her pace, determined not to let anything interfere with her pursuit of a bath and a bed. Sadly, her feet moved away, but her curiosity strayed towards the trouble.

'Not so big . . . now . . . are you . . . Rudd?'

'Don't kill him, Sully. The boss said we was to watch him, check him out, that's all.'

Sully chuckled. 'Accidents happen though, right?'

Ros slowed at the mouth of a passageway running between a hotel and a saloon. Pale light flickering from windows illuminated four men exchanging brutal blows in a dispute the taller one looked likely to lose. Ros pressed against the wall, her sense of injustice fuelling her unvented anger as two of the men caught hold of Rudd and the third punched him in the stom-ach. When Rudd's knees finally buckled, a left hook sprayed blood from a gash above his eye.

'You boys are making a mistake. I'm a—' Rudd gagged, as he sprawled in the dirt.

Sully yanked him up by his hair. 'Mr Swain told us what you are. That's the whole point. Don't you get it? We don't want you coming in and interfering. Now stop whining and die.'

Sully pulled back his knee to ram it in Rudd's face and Ros backed away, wary of getting involved, yet unable to leave a man to possible death. *Damn it*! It was none of her business. She should turn around and walk away. That's what she should do.

Instead, she shouted gruffly, 'Hey, what's going on?'

Three dirty faces turned, distinct only by their increasing degrees of ugliness.

'Get out of here, kid,' Sully snarled.

Rudd groaned, earning himself a kick in the ribs. This time he rolled onto his side and lay quiet.

'He's had enough.' Anger boiled inside Ros but she managed to keep her tone conversational. 'What's he done?'

'Why, do you want some, boy?' Sully shouted.

Obscured by shadows and dressed in dark pants and a range coat there was no way they could tell she was a woman. Her hair shoved up under her hat, and a voice husky from eating dust, strengthened the disguise. If she was lucky, these cowards might run from a man with a gun. Dropping her saddle-bags, she slipped her hand inside her coat, touching the Colt holstered at her waist.

'You're getting involved in something that doesn't concern you.' Sully booted Rudd in the back. 'We don't like that.'

She drew the Colt and cocked the hammer. 'Well, I don't like to waste my bullets, but if you don't walk away from here I'll drop you where you stand.'

They laughed. 'Is that so? Well, we say you won't 'cause there's three of us and one of you.'

Confidence in her ability surpassed any fear. 'I think you're forgetting my six friends.'

She dived behind a pile of trash, spraying bullets until the pistol clicked. Shots kicked-up dirt around her as she scooped a handful of ammunition from her pocket, emptied the spent shells and refilled the empty chambers. Again, she opened fire.

'I'm hit!' Sully's squeal marked the end of the onslaught. 'Barclay, where are you?'

'I took one in the leg,' Barclay screamed. 'Shorty, did you get him? Shorty. Shorty!'

Ros waited. She hadn't wanted to kill anybody but what else had she expected sowing bullets like chicken feed?

'Gotcha!'

Her gun skittered away, jarred out of her hand by a blow that numbed her arm and knocked her further into the shadows. She swiped for her hat as it spun off, but an arm locked around her throat and stopped her with a painful jerk. Like a barroom brawler, she clawed, frantically trying to clear her windpipe as she was dragged through the mud on her knees.

'Well, lookee here. Shorty got himself a female at last.' Sully stumbled towards her, blood pouring from a shoulder wound. 'Hell. That means I've been shot by a woman. Bitch! You're gonna pay for this, girly.'

Ros choked short gasps of air as Shorty released his grip and yanked her elbows behind her back. For a second, she glimpsed knuckles then blood filled her mouth as fog descended over her eyes. She let it consume her but the reprieve was short-lived when Sully's rank breath shocked reality back into focus.

'I'm going to teach you a lesson you won't forget,' he growled.

She spat in his face, reeling when another blow glanced off her cheek.

'Leave her alone, Sully. It's me you want.'

'Stay down, Rudd. You'll get what's coming to you soon enough.'

'Help me. . . .' Ros's throat burned.

'Get down,' Rudd shouted.

Boom! Sully lifted like a puppet on strings. Shorty's grip faltered. Ros dived, covering her ears as one roar, then another, deafened her. She lay still, waiting, afraid to breathe, powerless to move, as voices echoed beyond the passageway – people shouting, running, shooting.

Panic gripped her. What if *they* were coming, too?

She scrambled, helped by somebody grabbing her under the arm, then recognized Rudd's voice. 'Come on, let's get out of here.'

'My gun,' she said, raking the ground.

Already people were flooding in behind them. Someone shouted 'Murder' and called for the sheriff. The Colt touched her palm and her fingers closed around it as Rudd pulled her into deeper cover.

'Wait, my gear's back there.'

She tried to go back but Rudd yanked her elbow.

'Forget it. Those three probably have friends in that crowd and I don't want to end up with a bullet in my back or a rope around my neck.'

She hesitated. Her money was in those bags. *Oh, what the hell.* It wasn't worth her life. She ran blindly until he shoved her into a hotel lobby where the glow of a lantern hid none of the décor's shabbiness or years of neglect that had left the wooden floor scarred and dirty.

Rudd wrapped his arm around her waist. 'Let me do the talking.'

She ducked her head, spraying hair across her face just as the thin clerk peered up from the book he was reading.

'Looks like you had a good night, Mr Rudd.'

Coins clinked as they landed on the high desk. 'You should see the other feller.'

Laughter followed them as they mounted a flight of stairs then hurried along a dimly lit passage. At the end, Rudd unlocked a door and disappeared into darkness. Ros waited outside, rubbing her throat where the imprint of Shorty's fingers still burned. A moment later, a flame sputtered, illuminating Rudd.

'Are you coming?'

Ros glanced inside, noticing the garish wallpaper and the stale air a second before Rudd tugged her in. Before she could argue, he slammed the door, wrapped her in his arms and kissed her.

'I don't know where you came from and I don't care,' he muttered. 'You're alive. I still can't believe it, but here you are, Ros.'

She played along, long enough to slip the Colt out. Firmly, she pressed the muzzle into his ribs. 'Hold it right there, mister, or I'll finish what Sully started.'

CHAPTER 2

She slipped his gun out of its holster and jabbed him in the side until he moved back. 'How do you know me?'

Rudd smiled. 'What do you mean?'

'Answer the question.'

He sat down on the edge of the bed, looking more uncertain than worried. 'You are Ros, aren't you?'

'Maybe. Let's just find out who you are before we get too friendly.'

'You're kidding me.'

She held the weapon steady, aiming at his chest. 'I see your mouth moving, Mr Rudd, but you're not making any sense. Maybe them fellers hit you harder than you thought.'

'All right, let's start again. My name's Jake. Jake Rudd. Can you at least lower the gun?' He smiled disarmingly. 'Even if you don't recognize me, I promise you, I never touched any woman who didn't want me to.'

She searched her memory for the name as she looked him over. He was tall, at least six feet, and his big hands hanging loose at his sides had felt soft and supple, not rough like a cowboy or a farmer's. She thought about the gun in her hand. An 1873 Colt with a seven-and-a-half inch barrel – not an obvious gunfighter's choice, although the handle was smooth against her palm, well used.

'Do you like what you see?' he asked.

She wetted her lips, playing out her blatant consideration like the seasoned whore she imagined he thought she must be. 'Tall, dark, eyes the colour of whiskey, and wearing a handmade suit . . .' Whatever the reason for her madness, she tossed him the six-shooter. 'What's not to like?'

He caught the gun and slid it back in its holster, replacing the thong. 'You're direct. I'm not sure I approve.'

She was too tired to argue. 'Makes no difference to me.'

His breath whistled as he sucked it in. 'Ros, is that any way to greet an old friend? Have you really forgotten me, or are you just as surprised to see me standing here, breathing, as I am to see you?'

For a split second, she wondered if he'd been a friend of the sisters, but he'd talked about being surprised to see her alive and that meant he had to have known her from a time before she joined the mission.

'Nothing much surprises me, Mr Rudd,' she said, keeping a tight rein on her curiosity.

'Sure seems that way. Look, I don't blame you for shooting me, if that's what you're worried about.

12

Knowing what you and me had, there was no way you would have sold me out.'

He made no sense but she wasn't in the mood for an explanation. 'You don't look shot and I don't know what you're talking about and I don't want to know. If you're so ready to forgive and forget, let's just say I don't have a good head for names or faces and leave it at that.'

She tossed her coat onto the only chair in the room and stalked to the window. Peering through a gap in the tattered curtains, she studied the saloon opposite where two men played cards at a table by the door. Nearby, someone banged a lively tune on a piano and a chorus of drunken voices joined in. Looking further along the street, she noted the sheriff's office where a light glowed between closed shutters.

'It doesn't look like we were followed,' she said, bumping into Rudd as she turned.

He seemed anxious to be close to her, but he stepped aside. 'I doubt anybody saw us come in here. We should be safe until I can straighten things out.'

She wondered how he intended to 'straighten out' three dead bodies but a wave of tiredness washed over her before she could draw a conclusion. Irritably, she rubbed her eyes and pushed past him.

'Do what you have to, Mr Rudd. I'm way past caring.'

'Looks that way. How long is it since you slept?'

She wasn't sure, but as she threw herself down on the creaky bed, she didn't expect it to be much longer. 'A day or two,' she said as her eyes closed under the weight of their lids. 'Just so you know, I'm taking you at your word, Mr Rudd, and staying 'til morning.'

'Make yourself at home. I need to go out for a while.'

His voice moved around the room but Ros didn't hear him take a step. She forced one eye partway open in time to see him pull a roll of money from his waist-coat. He peeled off five dollars and slipped it back. The remainder, about fifty judging by the bulge, he slid down the inside of his boot before snugging his pant's leg over the top.

Her mind jumped back to the fight. 'What was that beating all about?'

'Dunno, but they knew who I was. Probably just somebody with a grudge.' He looked up. 'Sorry you got caught up in it. You're going to have a few bruises.'

She fingered the spot on her cheek where Sully's knuckles had done their damage. 'Might turn out to be a good thing, make me less easy to recognize, give me some time.'

Rudd arched a brow, but a commotion in the hall-way stalled any questions he might have asked. They each grabbed for their gun. He was faster. When their stares met, the cold glint in his eyes challenged her. Rightly or wrongly, she didn't believe he'd kill her, even though she was sure he could.

The noise faded away and Rudd cracked open the door to peer out.

'Just a drunken neighbour.'

A wink softened the killer she'd glimpsed a few moments before, and with that, he opened the door wide enough to slip out and was gone.

'It's a thin line you walk, and one of these days you'll cross it. When you do, that badge you're hiding in your pocket won't help you one damn bit.' The steam rising from the sheriff's cup fogged his spectacles and he slipped them to the end of his nose as he continued to study Rudd. 'Next time, it'll be you dead with a bullet in your back instead of three no-accounts.'

Jake continued to lean against the wanted-posters board, idly flicking between layers of paper while he waited for the sheriff to finish his tongue-lashing.

'Have a thought for an old friend, will you, Jake? It's been a while since I wore my burying suit and it needs to be a while longer yet.'

The sheriff's thinly veiled concern touched him and he chuckled. 'You worry too much, but at least I know there'll be one mourner at my funeral.'

A grunt suggested that might be true. 'It's no laughing matter, Jake. It's been a long time since I known anybody to get the jump on you. What happened?'

'I was careless.'

Riley quirked a bushy eyebrow. 'I doubt you even know what that means. Anyhow, you said there was a woman. What was it, nice smile or appealing assets?'

'More like a ghost.'

'Come again? For a minute there, I thought you said a ghost.'

'I did. Did I ever tell you I was nearly married?'

Giving it some considerable thought, Riley scratched the tip of his nose. 'Nope.'

15

'Then let me tell you about her.' Jake shoved away from the wall and perched on the corner of the sheriff's cluttered desk. 'I met her about four years ago, about a year after I hooked up with you. She got under my skin the minute I laid eyes on her.' He couldn't finish. Even now, he remembered how everything else paled compared to her red hair and blue-green eyes.

'Then why don't I know her?'

'It all happened around the time you were in Texas trying to round up the Quentin Gang. You were gone about six months, as I recall. By the time you got back it was all over.'

'You mean she left you for another man?' the sheriff said, with a note of inevitability.

Jake bristled. 'She died.'

Riley knocked Jake's leg aside and opened a drawer. A quick rummage yielded a silver hip flask. 'I'm sorry to hear that, boy, but what's that got to do with you nearly getting killed tonight?'

'I was following her.'

'What? When? Jake, you're talking in riddles. Have a drink.'

Jake bridled at Riley's off-handedness but he kept his ire in check. Not that he would have bothered for anybody else. He would have just walked away. But Riley was an old friend. Old. In the time since Jake had last seen him, the lawman had aged ten years. His hair was thinner and greyer and he'd lost weight. He looked tired, not just weary, but worn out.

Nonetheless, Jake had a lot of respect for him and he remembered that as he levelled his tone. 'She

16

walked into town about an hour ago. I wasn't sure it was her at first but . . .' He pictured her, but not in the range clothes she wore now, in something a little more revealing. 'Let's say, she seemed familiar and I wanted a closer look.'

'But how could it be?'

'I don't know, but she's here.' He smirked, recalling the calculating way she'd looked him over as though he was a thoroughbred horse or a custom-made pistol. 'She was a pretty kid, but she's a beautiful woman. Wherever she's been, it looks like life's been kind to her.'

Riley scratched his head. 'So what did she have to say for herself?'

'Nothing. Acted as though we never met before.'

'Are you saying she doesn't know who you are?'

Regret overshadowed Jake's good mood and he nodded.

'What are you aiming to do about that?' Finally, the sheriff sounded interested.

'Help her remember. To tell the truth, that's the least of my worries.'

'It is?'

'She's running scared. I'm not going to let her down this time.' Jake noticed a sudden frown driving deep furrows into his friend's brow. 'What?'

'I'm just not sure you've thought this through. Three years ago you were a different person. The past ain't always a good place to revisit, especially when you killed a man to put it behind you. What about Parley Jones and Jay Langerud? Have you thought about them?'

17

Jay Langerud, a fast gun with a reputation. Jake hadn't thought about him in a long time. He didn't welcome the image that flooded his mind of a body lying face down at the bottom of a ravine with buzzards circling.

He shrugged it away. 'I always expected the past to catch up with me, Riley. To tell the truth, I thought it would've happened sooner. You can only borrow time for so long.'

'True, but do you think this woman's worth risking the life you've carved out for yourself?'

Jake smiled. 'Riley, she's the only thing worth risking my life for.'

CHAPTER 3

After undressing quickly and removing the bindings around her breasts, Ros slipped into bed. Despite her screaming tiredness, a dozen questions refused to let her sleep. Mainly, they were about Rudd. Something about him was familiar, but whether he was friend or foe, she couldn't decide. Had he been the one following her when she left the livery? Was he another hired gun? *No.* She relaxed. If she believed that, she wouldn't be naked and unarmed in a room he'd paid for.

Still, he continued to worry her, or maybe it was her willingness to trust him that really bothered her. He was too at ease with himself to be a hired killer, she argued. More than likely he was a gambler and those three who'd set on him were mean losers. Yes, a gambler . . . slick . . . fast with a gun . . . no threat to her she decided as she drifted off.

Jake got back around midnight hoping to talk but the snores that greeted him put paid to that idea. He decided to let Ros sleep, despite the arousal her nakedness caused before he pulled the edges of the blankets over her. He couldn't trust himself to join her and settled into the chair by the door. Like the rest of the hotel the furniture had seen better days and after half an hour fidgeting, Jake gave up the pursuit of sleep and let his mind loose to wander.

It had been a long day and in all the excitement he'd forgotten to ask Riley what was so important that he'd had to drop everything and travel halfway across Kansas and Colorado. Maybe forgotten wasn't quite the truth. Maybe he just didn't want to know since, until tonight, trouble had been avoiding him and he kind of liked it that way. Experience told him Riley's wire could only mean an end to that peace.

He banged his elbow again and resigned himself to a sleepless night. Stalking irritably to the window, he scowled into the street. A dog crossed the road, but nothing else stirred and his attention fixed on the saloon opposite where lights glowed with a bright invitation.

Could he risk showing himself in a saloon? Maybe not, but Riley had a flask. No, it was too late to disturb him. Besides, there was still the question of who had sent Sully and his cronies after him, and why. A saloon would be the best place to find out. Mind made up, he tiptoed to the dresser to collect his hat but Ros's gun lying beside it caught his eye. Carefully, he slipped it from its holster and moved closer to the light.

'Pretty. Colt Peacemaker. Solid silver handle. Inlaid with mother of pearl.'

He spun the chamber, listening to the smooth action, then weighed it on his palm. It slipped easily into firing position, impressing him with its balance and feel. It was a nice weapon. Clean. Ready for action.

A groan startled him and he glanced towards the bed as Ros rolled onto her side. He waited for her to settle then let out his breath, surprised to realize he'd been holding it. Turning his attention to the Colt, he slid it back into the holster, feeling suddenly uncomfortable. Women shouldn't carry guns. They sure as hell shouldn't know how to use them. Jay Langerud had a lot to answer for teaching her that particular trick.

'I'm sorry, Ros. What happened in Hays was meant to be the beginning, not the end. I promise you I won't make the same mistake twice.'

There was no response and he hadn't expected one. He picked up his hat and turned down the lamp, needing a drink more than wanting one.

Ros waited for a click to signify Rudd closing the door, then swung her legs off the bed. She'd only been half-aware of him moving around until he mentioned Hays. That had woken her up as effectively as a bucket of cold water and unleashed a few more questions. Like, had he had something to do with her accident? Was he the one who'd pushed her in front of that stagecoach?

Squinting through one eye, she searched the semi-darkness for her clothes and spotted them on the dresser. Quickly she bound her breasts and finished dressing. To the east, a train whistle shrilled, stopping her as she fastened on her gun-belt. She listened to the steady chug of the engine growing louder. She'd prefer not to travel tonight, but whatever Rudd's motives were, she couldn't risk waiting. Not only that, but without money, catching a midnight ride in an empty boxcar was probably her only option.

She looked around for her hat, remembering she'd lost it, then snatched the door open. *No*. She couldn't risk meeting Rudd, and if the desk clerk saw her he might get word to him. She closed the door as if she were handling dynamite then moved stealthily to the window. Easing it open, she paused a moment to let the gentle breeze cool her cheeks, then after a quick glance along the street, she looked down, swaying as the boardwalk shimmered beneath her. After a few seconds, she climbed onto the window ledge, turned and swung her legs down. Lowering herself to arm's length, she dropped. It felt as if she'd done it a thousand times and she met the ground with cat-like grace, landing on the balls of her feet then effortlessly shifting her weight to her hands and knees. Without a pause, she sprang into the shadows and ran.

A couple of turns later, she spied a light shining from the stationmaster's office. She hunkered down in the shadows to wait and within moments a dozen freight cars screeched to a stop and a guard jumped down onto the platform.

'All right, Monty? Didn't expect to see you tonight,' he shouted, when the stationmaster lumbered out to meet him. 'Heard the news then?'

'Heard my wife say she'd shoot me in my dumb ass if I forgot to give you your sister's birthday present this time through,' Monty said, drily. 'You're late, Clyde.

You were supposed to be here four hours ago.'

'We ran into some trouble. Had to make an unscheduled stop.' The guard swung his lantern high and peered inside the first boxcar before sliding the door shut and moving to the next.

'What kind of trouble?'

'A body on the track.'

'What kind of body?' Monty asked, keeping close.

A prolonged creak preceded a gush of water as the driver refilled the engine. Clyde shouted over the sound. 'A dead one. A woman.'

Using the darkness for cover, Ros followed the two men, morbidly eager to hear the details.

'Did she throw herself in front of the engine?' Monty asked.

'No. The sheriff said it looked like murder. She'd been shot in the back, stripped naked and left on the tracks as though whoever did it, didn't want her found.' Clyde checked inside the penultimate car. 'Funny thing though. Whoever it was, they scalped her.'

'What!'

Monty's shock matched Ros's and she barely covered her mouth in time to keep from echoing it.

'You heard me right,' Clyde said slamming the door and leading Monty back towards the office. 'I bet she was pretty too. Had a face full of freckles and you just know she was a feisty little redhead.'

CHAPTER 4

In the early hours of the morning, Jake let himself into the sheriff's office. He found Riley asleep in a cell and nudged him.

'You awake, old man?'

Without opening his eyes, the sheriff rolled out of his cot and let himself out of the otherwise vacant accommodation. Stretching and yawning, he pulled up his sagging britches and kicked his feet into his boots before staggering to the stove. He was halfway through a cup of coffee before he opened his eyes.

'What are you doing back here so soon? Kick you out again, did she?' he asked, slurring his words and struggling to tuck his shirt in. 'What time is it anyway?'

'Past midnight.' Throwing a log into the stove, Jake settled himself into the sheriff's chair and crossed his ankles on the desk. 'You still got that flask handy?'

It appeared in Riley's fist with a sleight of hand that baffled Jake.

'What's wrong with yours?' Riley asked, pouring some in a cup and handing it over.

'I gave it up,' Jake said flatly. 'I just went back to the

hotel and Ros is gone, out the window I reckon.'

Riley's breath whistled as he sucked it in knowingly. 'You must be losing some of your charm.'

Jake stared into his cup, too caught up in his thoughts to indulge the sheriff's attempted humour. 'I know she didn't have any money, she admitted that much. The livery owner told me she sold her horse and saddle. She must have skipped out on the freight train that came through. The question is, why?' He ran his fingers through his hair as if trying to extract an answer. 'What's she running from?'

'How do you know she's running from anything? Maybe she just had to be someplace else.'

'Look,' Jake snapped, 'I might not be wearing my badge but that doesn't mean I've stopped being a lawman, or thinking like one. I told you, she's in trouble.'

Riley grimaced. 'I'll take your word for it, son, but did you stop to think that maybe you don't want to get mixed up in it? Before you even knew for sure who she was, she nearly got you killed.'

Jake grunted, unconvinced and unwilling to blame her for his stupidity. The only thing was, if he thought about it he might start to agree.

Riley poked him in the shoulder, startling him from his misgivings. 'Are you listening?'

'No,' he said, sullenly.

The sheriff rolled his eyes. 'I was saying, what you need is a job to do, give yourself time to think things over.'

Suspicion narrowed Jake's eyes. 'I take it you have

something in mind.'

'Well, now you ask, yes.' The sheriff hesitated, obviously weighing Jake's reaction. 'What do you know about Langley?'

Only half listening, Jake drained his cup and pushed it into a pile of papers on the desk. 'Never heard of it before your letter caught up with me, and so far I haven't had time to form an unbiased opinion.'

'Don't surprise me. It's a cattle town. Not too big. It's got a couple of hotels, two or three saloons, a general store, a schoolroom. The railroad arrived about six months ago, but we don't get many visitors. That's about it if you don't mention the richest cattle spread for two hundred miles.' Riley poured whiskey into his cup. 'Around a hundred and fifty folks or thereabouts call it home. It's a nice place, or was, but it's turned nasty. A feller by the name of Emmett Swain is muscling in, taking over the territory, seems like.'

Jake recognized the name. Sully had mentioned it.

'A newcomer?' he asked.

'Not exactly. He's from around these parts, but he's been away. Got back a couple of months ago and opened up a can o' worms. It's an old feud of sorts, between him and a local rancher.'

'What kind of feud?'

'What kind? Fence cutting, cattle rustling ... murder.'

Jake's concentration waned. Most of what Riley said was hardly noteworthy. Fence cutting had been widespread since the introduction of barbed wire and where there were cows there'd always be rustlers.

'Why don't you let them get on with it? These things usually sort themselves out, don't they?'

'Maybe, but this town's dying. The word's getting around. There's already talk about the railroad pulling out.' He shook his head. 'Pretty soon all that'll be left is a cemetery with some interesting markers.'

Jake shrugged, reluctant to ask his next question. Riley had cleverly skirted the issue of the shootings, but there couldn't be any other reason he'd want his help. He waited, but the silence irritated him.

'What's any of that got to do with me? You know I work behind a desk these days.'

'And you hate paperwork. Besides, this is more a favour to me.'

Jake's loyalty made him raise an eyebrow, inviting Riley to tell him more.

'Swain's bringing in hired guns.' Riley's shoulders slumped and he circled his fingertip around the rim of his cup. 'I ain't a young man, Jake. Maybe I could have handled this kind of trouble ten years ago, but I'm just too old. Truth is, I can barely see three feet in front of my face these days.'

Jake held up his hand and nodded. The fewer bleeding-heart details he had the better. 'I get it, Riley. You want to bring in a hired gun of your own.'

The sheriff fetched himself another coffee. 'You and me go back a long way, Jake. I wouldn't ask if it didn't mean a lot to me. What do you say?'

It hurt Jake to deny his friend, but he had a lot of ground to make up with Ros, if he could find her again. Not to mention she couldn't have walked back into his life at a better time, what with a letter of resignation making its way to the governor's office. Getting mixed up in somebody else's war could tie him up for months, after which time, she'd be long gone.

He stood abruptly, sending the chair rolling across the floor as he headed for the door. 'I need a day or two to think it over,' he said, more to himself than Riley.

'Jake, I kinda thought—'

Pausing in the doorway, Jake didn't bother to turn. 'I said, I need to think it over.'

'I heard you. I just hope you know what you're doing.' Riley started back towards the cells. 'If you change your mind, there are a few folks I'll need to introduce to you.'

Jake didn't feel inclined to go back to an empty room, but raucous laughter and a tinny piano kept him away from the saloon. He visited the train station for a second time, looking for evidence Ros had been there, found nothing, walked around town for an hour, finally treading a heavy path back to the hotel.

The clock in the lobby struck two as he passed by the sleeping clerk and crept upstairs. A chorus of contented rumbles and snores marked his passage along the dimly lit hallway, only adding to his discontent. By the time he unlocked the door and stumbled into his own room, his spirits were as low as a bummer's heels.

Allowing his eyes time to adjust, he scanned the darkness, pausing a moment before shuffling to the bed. Keeping his movements nice and easy, he sat and removed his boots. Despite the cold, he didn't bother turning back the blankets. It was nothing unusual. Sleeping in his clothes was a habit, something he did when he wasn't sure what his next move would be.

Just to be careful, he drew his gun and, keeping hold of it, he rested it flat across his belly. Then with his hat tipped across his forehead, he wedged his elbow behind his head and closed his eyes.

'What made you come back?' he asked.

He'd spotted Ros, or someone he felt sure was her, standing in shadow by the window. She didn't speak for a long time but her breathing reached him, heavy and ragged, as though she was crying. Eventually, she sucked in a deep breath.

'I heard something that frightened me more than you. If it means what I think, the men who've been following me think I'm dead and I'll be safe here. The only question mark is you.'

He started to get up, ready to convince her she should trust him.

'Don't move,' she ordered. 'I've got my finger on the trigger of a Colt pointed in your direction and my hand's shaking. Even in the dark I doubt I'd miss at this range.'

Her monosyllabic tone chilled him and he remembered the last time she'd put a bullet in him. It had been meant for someone else, but that knowledge didn't ease his anxiety now and he settled back down.

'That's better,' she said. 'I want to know about Hays. You said Hays was supposed to be a new beginning not the end. What did you mean?'

She was being direct again and he bucked against it. 'What do you think I meant?'

He heard a movement, the sound of a match, and blinked as lamplight flickered on the dresser. She adjusted the flame low, allowing it to cast only a dim light over the room. After replacing the chimney, she sat on the windowsill, crossed her legs and leaned her elbows on her knees, all the time keeping her eyes and the gun firmly on him.

'This is not a game to me, Mr Rudd, so I'll get to the point.' She looked at him along the muzzle of her gun. 'Are you here to kill me?'

For a few seconds, he stared at her, looking for the girl he'd known years before. But with the lamp casting ugly shadows across her bruised face, and the Colt held steady, it was a stretch for his imagination. Like it or not, this wasn't the Ros of old times, teasing him with empty threats. This woman was at the end of her tether, and experience told him that was a dangerous place to be.

Moving slowly, he took up his former position, hand forming a pillow behind his head. 'You know, I'm not. Why don't you lower that cannon and tell me what this is all about?'

The gun wobbled, then she lowered it and fixed him with a hollow stare.

'People have been trying to kill me for a long time, Mr Rudd. I don't know who and I'm not sure why, but I might need someone to trust and right now you're the only one I've met who even comes close to inspiring me.'

He resisted the urge to gloat. 'I'm glad I inspire you,

but trust works both ways.'

His candour seemed to knock her off guard. She opened her mouth to speak, to offer an argument maybe, closed it then tried again. 'What do you need to know?'

He hesitated, wondering if she was testing him, but he had nothing to hide, nothing new at least.

'Where've you been for the past three years?'

She swivelled on the ledge, resting her chin on her knees as she brought them into her chest. 'Saint Mary's Sanctuary.'

He recognized the name, if not the exact place. 'You're a nun?' He blurted it like an accusation.

'More likely a sinner paying penance,' she said, miserably.

Jake remembered laughter coming from a crowded blackjack table where she dealt cards. Quickly his thoughts strayed to a hotel room with the sheets on the bed still warm. She'd been a responsive lover, but she'd never been a sinner.

'For what?' he asked.

'I don't know.' She ran a shaky hand through her hair, revealing more clearly the cavern of deep scars criss-crossing her forehead. 'Maybe you can tell me some time, but not now. I'm too tired to think.'

'You're welcome to half the bed.' He closed his eyes, wary of driving her away again if he pressed too hard. 'I never touched—'

'Any woman who didn't want you to.' The bed dipped as she slipped on beside him. 'And I never shot any man who didn't deserve it – probably.'

31

Jake was dreaming about blue-green eyes, red hair and creamy skin when a movement in the hallway snapped him awake. He pushed his hat away from his face and accustomed his eyes to the semi-darkness. Ros lay pressed against his side, snoring lightly. She stirred when he eased his legs off the bed to slip his feet into his boots.

'What's wrong?' she asked on a whisper.

He cocked his gun. 'Probably nothing. Go back to sleep.'

In a blur of movement and noise, the room exploded. Jake shoved Ros clear a split second before the door left its top hinge and crashed into him. It partly pinned his leg against the bed and, as he struggled to get free, a man's voice boomed into the room, 'You shoulda stayed dead, bitch.'

Jake's mouth tasted dry as cotton as he returned fire, aiming towards the flashes coming from the shadowy hallway. Then, as suddenly as it started, the onslaught stopped.

Cocking his revolver, Jake ran to the empty doorway, peering out before launching himself into the open. The passageway was empty. He started towards the stairs but a breeze on his back drew him to a window overlooking the street. There was blood smeared along the sill. He leaned out, hanging precariously across the ledge, but all was still.

As he backed inside, cussing, a commotion brought him round sharply, gun raised towards several lamps blinding him with sudden brightness. Doors on either side opened and bleary-eyed men wearing an assortment of underwear and nightshirts stumbled out.

'What the hell was that all about?' a fat man grumbled.

'Sounded like a gunfight to me,' mumbled another, winding a pair of spectacles around his ears. 'I asked for a quiet room when I signed in. I'm going to speak to—'

'No trouble, gents. You just go back to bed and forget about it.'

Jake recognized the high tone of the morning desk clerk, Eugene, a thin, balding man with bad skin and crooked teeth.

Jake holstered his pistol. 'Not so fast. Did anybody see anything?'

'I just heard a ruckus and got up to see what was going on,' Eugene whined.

The others mumbled their agreement.

'You better have a nice bank balance to back up them fancy clothes you wear, mister,' Eugene said. 'Like it says in the *foy-er*, all breakages must be paid for.'

The clerk's attempt at menace didn't worry Jake. There was nothing worth more than a dollar in the whole place. 'Go back to bed,' he ordered, spinning on his heel. 'We'll straighten this out later.'

Sidestepping the splintered door into his room, he moved towards the lamp on the dresser. The wick sputtered as he brought the flame up, but nothing else stirred.

He looked around. 'Ros, you can come—'

Her legs protruded beyond the foot of the bed on the far side and a closer look revealed Ros face down, blood spreading across the floor around her head. She was trying to push herself up.

'Son-of-a-bitch,' she complained, as Jake turned her over and hauled her onto the bed. 'I think you broke my nose.'

Ros tensed, unable to focus as breathtaking pain spread from her nose and ricocheted around her body. Rudd's quick thinking had almost certainly saved her life, but right now she wondered whether she'd ever breathe right or stand straight again. He'd slammed her down so hard she thought she'd suffocate. The sensation had seemed familiar and frightening, but in keeping with the other memories she had, it was indistinct.

Jake tipped her head back and pressed a towel against her face while he dabbed at her shirt with the edge of a blanket. She let him. Usually she picked herself up, but it was comforting to have someone else do it for a change.

'Let me look at you,' he said throwing the towel down and peering into her face. 'I'm no doctor but I don't think it's broken. Are you hurt anywhere else?'

She tried to flex her fingers, but a lightning sharp pain in her wrist and thumb paralysed her. 'Beats me how I hurt my hand when I stopped the fall with my face. I guess I should thank you for at least not killing me, but you'll forgive me if I don't do that right away.

Did you see who it was?'

'No, but I don't think he'll be back in a hurry. There was blood on the windowsill.'

Ros pointed past him to a sack half-hidden behind the splintered door. 'What's that?'

'Beats me,' Jake said, straightening the door on its remaining hinge before he retrieved the sack.

He held it as though it was a bag of rattlers, gingerly untying the knot in the top, then peeping inside. His nostrils flared as though the stench of rotting flesh was in his nose, his mouth tightening with revulsion as he reclosed it and threw it in the hallway.

'What was it?' Ros's hand trembled, her stomach clenching as she recalled the story the train guard had told about the body on the track. 'No, don't tell me.'

'You know, don't you?'

She clenched her chattering teeth and nodded, willing her knees not to knock as she squeezed them together. 'A scalp . . . with hair like mine.'

'Is that what you heard about that scared you more than me?'

She fought to control a new kind of fear. What if he decided not to help her? She had to know. 'I understand if you want to change your mind about helping me.'

Jake looked offended. 'If anybody can get you through this, I can. You've just got to trust me.' He pressed her down onto the bed and swung her legs up. 'I know it's hard, but try to get some sleep. There's nothing we can do now that we can't do later.'

She wanted to believe him, but Jake hadn't done anything to make her believe he was equal to blood-thirsty bounty-hunters and woman-killers.

CHAPTER 5

Something akin to gunfire startled Ros awake and she blinked rapidly, shying away from the direction of the window where a volley of rain lashed the glass. Pain gripped her in an instant and she groaned, unsure whether to roll over and suffer in silence or shoot herself and be done with it.

Rudd's arm tightened around her shoulder. When she glanced at his face, he appeared to be dozing. Judging by the daylight, the stiffness in her back and the sour taste in her mouth, she'd been asleep for a while. Somehow, she'd rolled onto his side of the bed and draped herself over him, using his chest for a pillow. It was a mistake, but she had to admit, she felt safer than she had in days.

'Are you awake?' she whispered.

'Of course.' His hand slid away from his pistol. 'How are you feeling?'

She sat up, bringing her knee between them as she spun to face him.

'Fine,' she said, lying as pain locked her hand.

She glanced at some swelling around her thumb

and wrist, but decided to worry about it later. Right now she needed an answer to at least one nagging question.

'Were you following me last night, or was it a coincidence that we met?'

Drawing his brows together, he tilted his head in a quizzical bird-like movement. 'Good morning to you, too.'

She dropped her focus to a new stain on the knee of her tan pants. 'Look, Mr Rudd, I want to trust you, but I don't know . . . Despite what happened last night – me saving your life, you saving mine – I need to know, is it you who's been following me? Either you were, or you weren't. It's a simple enough question.'

As he considered his answer, his natural sparkle seemed to dim, taking with it some of her optimism. Eventually, he got up and walked to the washstand, splashing his face with water before he continued. 'One that could take a while to answer honestly and, to tell the truth, I'm not inclined at the moment.'

'So you were.' Disappointment dulled the gratification she might have felt at being right.

'When you saved my life, yes, I'd followed you from the livery stable. When I came to town, no, that was coincidence. Or at least I thought it was.'

'You've changed your mind?'

'Uh-huh. You talk in your sleep. You kept saying 'Emmett Swain'.'

'I did?' she asked, trying to sound indifferent.

'Last night Sully mentioned that name, then later the sheriff said something about him.' He threw down the towel and faced her. 'Tell me about him.'

She searched her tattered memory. 'He's a man I was going to marry, a long time ago.'

A frown darkened his expression. 'How long ago?'

'I don't know, four or five years maybe. I don't remember everything before I woke up in the mission. Well that's not entirely true. Some things are still there but . . . just before the accident . . . that is to say; parts of my memory are a bit holey.' She swirled her finger against her temple.

'You mean you don't remember anything that happened in Hays?' He shook his head in disbelief. 'And that's something to do with the accident?'

'What do you know about that?' she snapped.

There was the slightest hesitation. Just enough to make her think his next words would be a lie.

'Just what I heard and things I read.' He smiled disarmingly. 'Of course, it looks as though the reports of your death were exaggerated.'

'Thanks to . . . the sisters at the sanctuary.' She stretched her back, hoping he wouldn't notice her white lie. 'I was as good as dead when they found me.'

'Found you? I don't understand. The accident happened in town, didn't it?'

'That's right, but from what I've been able to piece together, when I was taken to the doctor's house some-one had other plans for me. He patched me up then got a message that he had another patient to see across town. While he was gone somebody kidnapped me.'

Her voice cracked under the strain of recalling the cold-bloodedness of her abduction, although she had no true recollection of it. What she knew had been stitched together with information the girls had given her and things she'd found out in Hays just a few weeks ago. She saw no reason not to share the scant details

'They took me outside town and dumped me in the middle of nowhere, to die, with a bullet in my back for good measure.'

Rudd's knuckles turned white as his hands balled into fists. 'You don't need to say anymore about that. Tell me what happened after you left the sanctuary.'

Her breath formed a misty cloud, time dragging as she decided where to start. 'I went back to Hays, to the doctor who'd patched me up after the accident. I didn't know what else to do. Sadly, he'd died a few months earlier, but his wife remembered me. She had a few things of mine that he'd kept.'

'What things?'

'Nothing important, a stage ticket, a letter he found in my pocket.'

'His wife still had them after all that time? Why?'

Ros had asked herself the same thing. Now she just shrugged.

'She said her husband thought someone would come for them.'

Jake's attention seemed to wane as he gazed somewhere beyond her. Then, as if he'd been in a daydream, he said, 'Mind telling me what was in it?'

'It was more of a note really and it was faded.' She closed her eyes, her lips moving silently before she said, 'Marry me. It was signed *Jay*. I asked around but nobody knew what happened to him. I think he died.'

She let the detail sink in, trying to read Jake's expression, but he remained impassive.

'You said you knew me before, so what about Jay? Did you know him?'

Jake hesitated. 'No. Listen, I've got things to do. I need to ask around town, see what I can find out.'

She didn't believe him. He'd been firing questions like bullets until she mentioned Jay. For such an abrupt change to come over him, there must be something he wasn't telling her and she couldn't risk letting him leave before she had answers. On the other hand, she had no intention of begging.

'I'm sorry, I shouldn't ask you to tell me about another man. In fact, there's no reason why you should even get involved in my troubles.'

The ploy worked, drawing him into a denial.

'Believe me, there are at least a dozen reasons why I should get involved.'

'Like what?'

He took a minute. 'I lied to you. I let you believe I was something I wasn't, and when I should have trusted you, I lied again. If it hadn't been for my lies you wouldn't have—'

He left her with a hunger to know more that propelled her off the bed and pressed her face within inches of his. 'Everyone lies. With you it's more than that.'

'Now you're talking as if you know me.'

'Maybe I do.' She shook her head in denial. 'You seem familiar, as though I know more than I should about you.'

41

'That's an understatement.'

She stepped back from him, suddenly uncomfortable with their close proximity.

'We were lovers?' she asked.

He nodded.

'So why don't I recall your name?' She chuckled. 'I guess that answers one question I always had about my past. I was a whore.'

She didn't sound upset, more resigned to the truth.

'No, you weren't. We were more to each other than that.'

Before he could say more, she stalked to the window, looking for a distraction as she digested this new twist. It took a while.

'Did Jay know? Were you the one who killed him?' She didn't give him time to refute the accusation. 'Jake – Rudd.' She said it several times, chewing over the words like a delicacy. 'I wish I could remember you. There's something you're not telling me and I want to know what it is.'

'That's enough for now. The past ain't always a good place to revisit,' Jake said. 'You're just going to have to trust me. When the time's right, you'll remember.'

This time she decided not to argue but she couldn't resist throwing him one final challenge. 'You said you were a liar. Why should I trust anything you say now?'

'Because the truth might be more than you can handle, and I don't want another bullet in my back. Trust me, Ros. If you'd trusted me before, things would be a whole lot different now.'

CHAPTER 6

By the time he walked out of the hotel and into weak winter sunshine, the noon stage was just pulling up. He stopped in the doorway, waiting for a throng of passengers, friends and relatives to clear the area before he could continue. When he started on his way, someone tugged his sleeve, stopping him, and a child's voice asked, 'Can I help you, mister?'

Jake looked down into the grubby face of a boy no more than ten years old. 'With what?'

'Anything that'll get me the price of a biscuit at Peggy's café.'

Jake looked him over from his skinny shoulders to his bare feet, taking in the ragged britches and the frayed cuffs of his faded shirt. He needed more than a biscuit to put flesh on his bones and colour in his cheeks. Jake thought about giving him a few cents, but figured the way the kid's brown eyes bored into him, he wasn't looking for charity.

'My name's Jimmy McKendrick. I'm all right. Everybody knows me, mister. My pa killed hisself after

43

he lost our farm, so I run errands. Please, mister, I wouldn't cheat you.'

The boy's story was uncomfortably familiar, reminding Jake of a part of his life he preferred to forget. Yet meeting Ros again had already dragged him some way back towards it, and now this boy's plight brought more unhappy memories.

'All right, kid,' he said, shoving the similarities to the back of his mind. 'Go tell the sheriff to meet me in the saloon.'

He flipped a coin, watching the boy's freckled face brighten as he snatched the reward out of the air.

'What name shall I tell him, sir?'

'Rudd.'

Jimmy repeated it. 'I'll tell him, and if you need anything else just ask for Jimmy, that's me. Everybody knows where to find me.'

'All right, Jimmy, I'll remember. Now, do you know which way to the nearest saloon?'

Jimmy's smile disappeared, his hands balling into fists. 'Are you one of Swain's guns?'

Jake frowned. 'No.'

The kid's scowl transformed into a grin. 'Good, 'cause I kinda like you and he killed my pa. You watch out. He'll kill you too if you're not one of his kind.'

The boy was rambling, but from the moment he'd mentioned the name, he had Rudd's attention.

'His kind?' Jake asked trying not to sound too interested.

'Thief. Murderer. Liar. Cheat.' His chin trembled and he pouted. 'He killed my pa. He'd kill me too 'cept he don't think I'm big enough to worry over.' He chuckled. 'He's wrong though. I got a gun and I've been practising. One day I'll . . . I'll. . . .'

For all his big words, the tremor in Jimmy's voice betrayed his lack of conviction. Maybe when Jake had time, he'd sit Jimmy down and tell him about the trouble a gun and a big mouth could get him into. For now, he ruffled the boy's hair and slipped two more bits into his hand.

'When you've given my message to the sheriff, get yourself some eggs and bacon at Peggy's café, all right?'

Jimmy's shoulders straightened. 'Thank you, Mr Rudd. I'll be seeing you.'

Jake watched him sprint away, then turned and headed in the direction he hoped to find a saloon and some answers. A short distance and a bend in the main road found him within sight of the Crystal Slipper, but a freight wagon and an argument between an elderly woman and a smartly dressed young man blocked the sidewalk.

Jake tried to sidestep the pair, but the kid moved, unintentionally blocking his path with his back. Close up, the woman appeared ghost-like inside a black dress that barely skimmed her skeletal frame and her grey-flecked hair straggled in tangles around her shoulders. Jake thought about asking to pass, but the ferocity of the discussion ruled out an interruption.

'May, stop pushing me,' the man said. 'I don't want to talk about it and I'd appreciate it if you'd respect my wishes on that.'

The old woman seemed determined not to let it end. 'I'm sorry, Matt. I know it's hard for you to accept the truth about your sister, but she's dead. Why can't you accept it?'

'Because if she's really been dead all these years then it's time I started mourning.' He sucked in a breath. 'And I'm sorry, but with everything else that's going on, I don't have time for that right now.'

May tried to grab his arm. 'That's right, you don't have time. In fact, it seems you don't have time for anything anymore. Have you even considered what this is doing to Ava? Do you think she needs this worry in her condition?'

'That's a low blow, Aunt May. Ava understands me. Maybe you're the one causing all the worry. Did you think of that?'

She reeled as if he'd slapped her. 'I didn't know you felt that way.'

He shrugged it off. 'I don't. Just have a little faith, that's all I'm asking. She'll be back. You'll see.' He straightened his derby hat and stalked away.

Jake prepared to follow him, no longer trapped by them or the details of their argument, which he had to admit, intrigued him. There seemed to be a lot of dead women cropping up lately. But, just as he made a move, May walked into his path.

'Well, I don't share your blind faith,' she called after Matt's back. 'Wishing won't save the L. Someone needs to do something, and if you won't, I will.'

She turned abruptly, pushing past Jake and leaving the way clear for him to proceed to a much-needed drink. He paused to glance through a window before entering the saloon, a habit that had saved his life more than once. There was nobody he recognized inside, just two men in suits talking at a table, a cowboy at the bar, one tired-looking whore and the bartender.

Jake pushed through the batwing doors with a nod that acknowledged the glances that greeted him, then striding to the back of the room, he leaned on the freshly wiped bar and ordered whiskey. The bartender slid a glass in front of him and filled it without looking where he poured.

'On the house, stranger.'

Jake took a gulp, leaving a small amount in the bottom of his glass to deter a refill. 'Thanks.'

After a pause, the bartender corked the bottle and walked away to polish glasses, while Jake contemplated the remains of his drink. A chair scraped across the floor nearby and, raising his gaze slightly, Jake noticed the mirror over the bar offered a good view of the room. The two men sitting behind him had moved closer together, and instinctively Jake tuned his hearing to their hushed conversation.

'Look, Mr Swain—'

Jake focused on the back of the man sitting closest to him. His brown-striped suit accentuated broad shoulders and a wide back, and his oiled grey-brown hair looked freshly barbered. Relaxing in his chair and blowing smoke rings, he seemed unaffected by his companion's harsh tone.

'Take it easy, Radley. No need to get excited,' he said, calmly.

47

'That's all right for you to say. I did what you told me. I even brought you what you asked for.' Radley shook his head, something akin to disgust twisting his features. 'If you want me to do that again, I want double what you paid me this time.'

'You're lucky I'm paying you at all.'

'What the hell . . .' Radley slicked a palm over his close cut, blond hair, blinking rapidly as though the light hurt his ice-blue eyes. 'Don't you trust me?'

'Your friend Carson seems to think you might have been off the mark this time. He says she's in town.'

'I told you when I signed on that when I say I've done a job, it's done. I've never needed to notch my gun or take trophies. Carson's just sore that he's been chasing the wrong woman.'

'That's enough, Radley. I'm not paying you to talk . . . and this is not the place.' Swain glanced over his shoulder, his dark gaze meeting Jake's reflection in the mirror. 'Enjoying your drink, Mr. . . ?'

Jake turned, almost knocking over his glass as he recognized the gent who stared back at him. It had been a long time, and the man who called himself Swain had aged a decade in the last three years, but the black eyes and sneer were seared onto Jake's memory. His hand itched to pull his gun.

'Rudd. Jake Rudd,' he said, then held his breath, body coiled tight as a spring as he waited for a reaction.

Swain took his time looking him over. Finally, his gaze fixed on the gun at Jake's hip, and the corner of his mouth twitched. He reminded Jake of an excited child finding a stash of stolen candy.

'I'm Emmett Swain. What's your business in town?' Swain relit his cigarillo. 'Maybe there's something I can do for you.'

Jake relaxed. For now at least, the man he'd brought to justice for a string of violent stagecoach robberies, appeared not to recognize him.

'I'm just visiting,' he said, finishing off his drink.

Swain frowned through a puff of smoke. 'Anyone I know?'

Jake tensed again. Was Swain's friendliness just a little too forced? After all, a beard and an extra thirty pounds was hardly a disguise.

'Swain!' A woman's voice cut into the conversation. 'Get out here and face me, murderer.'

Jake glanced towards the street, then at Emmett Swain. For a brief moment, the man's composure seemed to slip. His drink sloshed onto the table. Did it reveal anger, or surprise? Just like years before, Jake couldn't read the man, and that made him dangerous.

Radley sprang to his feet, legs braced apart, back straight, his hand near the gun tied at his thigh.

'Easy, Radley.'

Swain stood up and straightened his jacket. He was taller than Jake remembered, probably a little under six feet. Time hadn't been kind to him and, as a shaft of sunlight slanted across his face, he looked closer to thirty-five than twenty-five.

'Looks as though we'll have to continue our conversation another time, Mr Rudd.'

Jake nodded but his nonchalance was wasted as Swain walked to the door and pushed into the street. Like a hungry dog, Radley followed, and behind him, Jake.

'Mrs West, what can I do for you?' Swain asked, solicitously.

As he sidestepped to the left of Swain, Jake recognized the old woman, May. She stood alone in the street, her hands hanging loosely at her sides, an aggressive snarl twisting her weathered features.

'I want you to get out of town,' she shouted.

Swain laughed.

'I'm only going to ask you once.'

'Well, Maybelle, I'm afraid I'm going to have to decline. Maybe it's you and Matt who should think about moving on.'

Her jaw flexed. 'You know that's never going to happen. My father-in-law built this town. We own the biggest spread in these parts. Do you think you can run us off, just like that?'

'Run you off – it sounds so . . . unpleasant. I'm just worried for you, that's all, now Bill's gone.'

'Don't you speak his name. Bill didn't deserve a bullet in his back, you murdering son-of-a. . . .' Words seemed to fail her.

'Careful, Maybelle.' Swain's tone sounded deliberately patronizing. 'Things have already been said and nothing's been proved. All I'm saying is, Bill was a good man, but do you think a boy like Matt can handle a ranch the size of the L?'

Maybelle strode forward, halving the distance

between her and Swain to less than ten feet. 'Matt's a good man too. He'll do just fine if you leave us alone.'

'Maybe I should talk to him. It's high time. Is he in town today?'

'He's got nothing to say to you.'

Swain hesitated. 'I hear he's wearing a gun these days.'

Maybelle staggered backwards as if she'd been hit. 'You'd like that, wouldn't you, to shoot him down? Would you do it yourself or get your paid gun to do it for you?'

Jake noticed Radley's fingers creep closer to his Colt. The movement alarmed him. What kind of man would think about drawing on a woman? Reflexively, Jake's hand covered his own weapon.

'I think you should go home, Maybelle. You're causing a scene.' Swain waved his arm wide, indicating the onlookers. 'Neither one of us wants this, and you're not well. You're still mourning.'

She laughed. 'Don't hide behind the frailty of a woman. I asked you a question and I want an answer. Are you going to leave town?'

Swain shook his head slowly, as though he regretted his refusal. 'I've got too much invested to—'

Boom!

Swain reeled, blood soaking his sleeve as he crashed into Jake.

Boom! Boom!

When Jake looked up, Maybelle lay dead in the dirt, the gun she'd used to shoot Swain lay at her side. Two

51

bullet wounds spread a stain across her chest. Shoving Swain off, Jake turned in time to see Radley slide his gun back into its holster.

CHAPTER 7

Gunshots exploded the morning, setting Ros's insides to trembling with renewed trepidation. For a second it made her forget the soreness around her nose and the appalled look of the desk clerk as he waited for her to cross the lobby.

'Sounds like another customer for the undertaker,' he said, easing onto his elbows as he leaned forward for a closer look at her. 'Seems to me there's a fight just about every day.'

Ros hurried for the exit but the clerk stopped her.

'You look familiar. Do I know you?' he asked. 'Come to think of it, you look a lot like Bill and Matt West. You wouldn't happen to be related. . . ?'

Ros didn't wait for him to finish. She had questions of her own without having to answer somebody else's. Stepping outside, she sucked in a breath of fresh air and shivered as a cold wind whipped inside her thin coat. Turning her head this way and that like an over-awed child, she started off, marvelling at the unfamiliar sights. The town had been a scattering of houses, a general store, a hotel and a barber's shop along Main

Street when she left. Now, it spread out in all directions, a patchwork of buildings that clamoured for her attention.

The only thing that remained the same was her uneasiness. Maybe it had been a mistake to return. *No.* She was here now and the sooner she made her peace with her father, the sooner she could leave. She picked up her pace, but the back of a crowd greeted her when she cleared the bend. Cursing, she started to skirt around, unwilling to negotiate the tightly packed group. But quick as a lasso around her neck, a familiar voice brought her to a stop.

'She was a gentle, defenceless woman. What right did you have to kill her in cold blood?'

Matt? An unexpected rush of excitement propelled Ros into the throng.

'First my father, then my brother and now my sister-in-law. Looks as though that just leaves me, Swain. Maybe we need to finish this now, once and for all.'

'Now just a minute, Matt.' *Emmett Swain?* 'I'm not wearing a gun. I've got a bullet in my arm and at least ten witnesses who'll testify she was anything but defenceless.'

A murmur of agreement hummed through the crowd.

'So, I guess I'll be waiting for a bullet in my back then.'

'You shouldn't talk to Mr Swain that way, boy.'

The new voice sent a chill through Ros, particularly since the speaker hardly raised his voice to convey his sinister intent. She shoved her way into the throng, dodging a sea of elbows and shoulders that seemed determined to stop her.

'Keep out of this, Radley,' Matt warned.

'I'm afraid I can't do that since Mr Swain's paying my wages, and if you kill him, where does that leave me?'

Like a cork from a bottle, Ros popped out of the tight knit crowd. For a moment, she hesitated, hardly recognising the man standing less than five feet in front of her, legs spread, back straight, hand hovering over the Colt hung low and tied to his thigh. When she'd last seen him, Matt had been a twelve-year-old kid, playing in the dirt and following her around like a stray dog. Now, wearing a dark-grey suit, he resembled a bank clerk, but there was no mistaking the clean-cut profile with its long, straight nose and strong jaw. Except for his dark chestnut-coloured hair and blue-green eyes, he was a dead ringer for their father.

Pulling herself up straight, she strode between Matt and the blond gunfighter.

'Ros?'

'Later, Matt,' she mumbled, as she glimpsed Maybelle.

She hadn't seen the woman since her wedding day. She'd been pretty with dark hair and a generous figure, unrecognizable from the corpse lying just inches from Ros's boot.

'Who the hell are you supposed to be?'

She faced the tall blond, chilled by the equal measure of humour and menace she saw in his ice-blue eyes. Casually, she slipped her right hand inside her coat, flicking back the edges to reveal the Colt.

'In answer to your original question, Mr Radley, the one where you asked what would happen if your boss got himself killed, I'd say that would leave you out of a job. I guess the question you need to ask yourself is: would you rather be dead?'

A buzz blanketed the crowd.

Matt tugged at her arm. 'What are you doing?'

'Saving your life. Let me handle this.'

Radley grinned, his stare never flickering from her face. 'It's all right, kid, I don't fight women – or mama's boys.'

'I told you, Radley, my business is not with you.' Matt rested his hand on his sister's back. 'And it's lucky for you that you don't fight women. This is one lady you don't want to come up against in a fair fight.'

Pride threatened to overwhelm Ros, but she subdued it.

'Radley, get back over here,' a smooth voice ordered. 'I want a few words with you.'

Ros's gaze flashed towards the saloon where a man swayed from the shadows. *Emmett?* Shock formed a knot in the pit of her stomach. Life had ravaged his handsome features, carving heavy lines around his eyes and at the corners of his mouth. The sun shone harshly off his oiled hair. Nothing about him was the way she remembered, except for the wide-mouthed smirk.

'Ros, I never expected to see you ... here.' He glanced towards Radley, as if to say 'I told you', then back at her. 'I guess Hell must be frozen over.'

Neither her flawed memory nor her absence had dulled the awe she felt. As his gaze passed over her leisurely, the years disappeared to reveal an impressionable sixteen-year-old girl. Only something was different. Was it resentment that narrowed his eyes to spiteful slits?

She smiled, wishing it didn't come so easy. 'Hello, Emmett. It's been a long time.' Her focus shifted to Radley who had returned to his master's side. 'I see you still enjoy collecting bugs.'

'Still pretty as a sunset.' Emmett's friendly façade faltered. 'And sharp as vinegar.'

It shouldn't matter, but his criticism cut deep as a knife. She nodded towards his arm where blood seeped through his fingers and spread along his sleeve. 'You should let Doc Bailey take a look at that,' she said, despising herself for showing concern to a man who, now she thought about it, had never shown any to her.

Emmett nodded, but a movement in the doorway behind him drew Ros's attention from further small-talk. She almost choked when she recognized the cut and fit of a handmade suit. Her gaze drifted higher, past the starched collar and beard-covered jaw, finally locking with eyes the colour of whiskey. Something stirred in her memory, the shadow of a name that begged to be remembered, and definitely not the name she knew him by today.

'Mr Rudd, I might not have saved your life if I'd known you were on the payroll of the man threatening my family.'

Ros's look challenged him but he didn't flinch.

57

Instead, he stepped forward and leaned against the hitching rail. 'I'm not on anybody's payroll. I just got here, same as you.'

She believed him.

'You two know each other?' Emmett asked through clenched teeth. 'Seems there's more surprises here than a tombola draw. I thought I recognized—'

'Now, hold on just a minute,' a new voice shouted behind Ros.

She staggered as Matt tugged her aside, making way for a wiry old man waving a shotgun. From his crazy white hair to his worn-out boots, he was a multi-coloured mismatch. Brown jacket patched and mended with blue squares on the elbows and at the shoulders. Pants that might have been black at one time, but now were closer to grey and painfully thin around the rear. A livid red shirt that served to inflame his mottled complexion. When he pushed open his coat to scratch his armpit, the shiny tin star pinned to his vest was no less surprising to Ros than the next words he uttered.

Bow-legged, he strode towards Rudd, shaking him warmly by the hand. 'Just so there's no misunderstanding, welcome to Langley, Marshal Rudd.'

CHAPTER 8

Jake's first thought was to hit the big-mouthed sheriff over the head. His next was to grab a horse and get out of this crazy town. Instead, he did the only thing that made sense amid the chaos. He walked out into the street, raising his hands and addressed the noisy crowd.

'All right, folks, now you know who I am I want you to go about your business. And somebody fetch the undertaker, and a doctor.' Behind him, he heard the sheriff working to persuade Swain and Radley to go inside. 'There's nothing more to see.'

A few low grunts marked the crowd's slow departure, no one wanted to miss the already heated argument between Ros and her brother.

'What was I supposed to do, Matt?' Ros snapped. 'May was lying dead on the ground. Pa's dead. Bill's dead. And then you . . . you stand there looking and sounding like Billy the Kid.'

Matt broke away. Despite challenging Swain, he seemed loath to continue a fight with his irate sister. Jake admired the boy for his self-control, especially knowing how mad he himself had been when Ros stormed into the fray.

'Marshal, there's no need for the undertaker. We'll be taking Maybelle's body home with us.' Matt said, his anger still evident in the flush mottling his cheeks. 'Unless you've got a problem with that.'

Jake heard the challenge, but he didn't see any conviction in the kid's eyes. To tell the truth, he looked scared to death. And why wouldn't he? He was just a boy, sixteen at the outside. Radley was a killer. Not to mention his sister being a madwoman.

'Easy, son. I'm just trying to help.'

Ros pushed between them, dwarfed by the height of both men, and squinted up at him. 'Really? By standing idly by while a woman was murdered, then letting a man like Radley go loose?'

She walked away, forcing him to follow. Luckily, for Matt, he sidestepped in time to avoid being floored as Jake pushed through him.

'Ros! Don't walk away from me. We're not finished.'

'Yes, we are,' she sang over her shoulder.

Grabbing the back of her coat, he yanked her around. 'Not until you tell me what you thought you were doing walking into the middle of a gunfight. Then, instead of trying to break it up, you challenge a killer to a showdown. You're crazy.'

'So, I'm crazy. Are you finished?'

'No.' He grabbed her elbow, yanking her hand from her pocket and holding it high. 'What about this? Your fingers are as stiff as a new glove. If he'd pulled his gun, you'd be dead right now. Didn't I teach you anything? You never start a fight you can't win.'

He tightened his grip and the pressure reignited her spark.

'I didn't ask for your help. Let me go and leave me alone, you—'

'Sis!' Matt gripped her other arm. 'You're causing a scene. Let's go.'

'Not until—'

'Now,' he insisted.

Jake smiled at the look of surprise that stalled her argument, but his amusement was short-lived.

'When did you start giving me orders, little brother o' mine?' she asked softly.

'When you lost your mind – and your manners. The marshal's right. What you did was crazy, and arguing about it won't change anything.' He nodded to Jake to let her go, holding her elbow while she composed herself, then ignored her and addressed Jake. 'I'll have my foreman Colly come fetch my sister-in-law's body, if that's all right with you.'

'That's fine, son. As for your sister, see if you can't do something about that temper.'

A grin brightened Matt's strained demeanour. 'Don't push your luck, Marshal. If I remember right, she actually never starts a fight she can't win and she's probably crazy enough to shoot you.'

Ros reined in her indignation as she walked beside Matt, struggling to keep up with his long strides. She resented his resolute scowl, fixed firmly on the ground.

'I'm not sorry, Matt,' she said, stumbling to keep

pace with him. 'What was I supposed to do, let you get yourself killed?'

A muscle flexed in his jaw but his mouth remained tight. His silence only made Ros more determined to continue the argument.

'Why are you so mad? Just tell me. Get it out in the open.'

He didn't look at her. 'Where have you been? Why didn't you send word? And what did you think you were doing back there?' He growled in frustration. 'What you did was . . . reckless. The marshal was right. Maybe you should try listening to him.'

She gasped despite her best efforts to let him say his piece.

'Oh, just forget it,' he mumbled, edging away from her. 'I forgot you never listen to anybody, do you? That's why you left in the first place.'

His words smarted like a slap in the face and she gripped his elbow more roughly than she intended. He stopped dead and for the first time, he met her head on, anger tensing every muscle in his pale face. It aged him and shocked some sense into her. She had known being home was going to be hard, but looking at a mirror image of their father, a man she'd destroyed by her selfishness, was going to kill her a little every day – if she let it.

'Matt, say what's on your mind.' Her tone was unnecessarily harsh. 'Life's too short for keeping ugly things inside.'

'You're right, life is too short. Too short for a lot of things.' He closed his eyes and inhaled, obviously composing himself. 'I'm barely seventeen years old and over the past few weeks I've lost my pa, my brother and my sister-in-law, the people who raised me. Don't walk back into my life if you're just gonna get yourself killed. It's not fair.'

She hadn't expected him to be so brutally honest. It humbled her.

'All right, I deserved that, but let's not fight. You went to a lot of trouble to get me back here, I thought you'd be happy to see me.'

A flicker in his eyes betrayed his vulnerability. Luckily, anything he'd been about to say was lost when a door opened nearby. They both looked round at the man who emerged wearing grey pants and a white shirt with the sleeves rolled up.

He hurried forward, stopping short despite the appearance of being eager to greet her. 'Ros? I don't believe it.'

'Hello, Tom. Is Ava still here?' Matt asked.

'She went back to the hotel.'

Matt stepped aside, already moving away as he continued. 'I'm sure you two have got a lot to talk about. I'll be back later.'

Ros let him go. Knowing her own temper, and guessing Matt took after her, it was better to let him cool off at his own pace. She smoothed her hair and turned her attention to Tom. 'Hello. How are you?'

A frown dulled his expression. 'Never mind me. You look like hell.'

'With the stiffness and the pain when you try to move

63

your fingers. . . .' Doctor Thomas Bailey flexed each of her fingers in turn. 'It's hard to say for sure, but I'd say at worst you've broken every bone in your hand. At best it's just a bad swelling.'

She couldn't contain a smile. 'Let's hope for that then.'

He stopped his examination and looked into her face. 'It's good to see you. A surprise, but a good one. Looks as though Matt was right not to give up on you. He never believed you were dead, even after we got word you were.'

'He didn't?'

'Everybody else gave you up years ago, but not him. Even I wasn't sure. Still, after what happened nobody would have blamed you for starting a new life. You could have dropped off the face of the earth, done anything, gone anywhere.'

Ros struggled for something to say. She'd disappointed so many people.

'That was a long time ago. I put it behind me the day I rode out of here. I didn't come back to dredge up the past.'

He looked pensive as he picked up a length of bandage from a tray on the table. 'You haven't changed if you don't think that's exactly what your being back is going to do.'

Silence separated them as he unwound and rewound a dressing. Despite her brave words, the past was charging back with a vengeance.

'Tom, what's been happening? I see a personal in a newspaper, so I come back and walk into a gunfight between my baby brother and a hired killer. And what was Maybelle doing going after Emmett with a gun?'

'Maybelle?'

'She's dead. She tried to kill Emmett.'

Tom staggered. 'I can't believe it. Ava said she was finding it hard, but . . . it's an ugly business. Since your pa died and then Bill . . .' For a moment, words failed him. 'It's Swain's doing. He turned up a few months ago, a rich man, started trying to take over the town. He bought out a small farm here and there, then ranches, stores, the hotel. He owns mostly everything now except for—'

'The Circle Double L. Son of a—' She glanced sheepishly at him. 'Sorry, Tom. I've been keeping mixed company lately, although I think that particular slip of the tongue comes from a time I can't actually remember.'

'How much time?' He asked with obvious interest.

'I don't know, about six months – a year maybe.'

He nodded as though he understood. 'I read in a journal that sometimes that happens with a serious head wound, that the events nearest in time to the accident that caused the amnesia get lost.'

'You mean I'll never remember?' she asked. 'There's no cure?'

He shrugged. 'Nobody can say for sure. Something intense might spur your memory, I guess. Going back to the L, seeing Emmett again . . . you're right, he is a . . .' He paused to let her fill in the rest. 'Have you spoken to Matt about what's been happening?'

She picked at a thread on her sleeve. 'He seems very

independent. Why don't you fill me in?'

Tom started clearing away his instruments. It was a habit, something she remembered he did to avoid awkward situations. Ros followed him, standing firmly in his path when he tried to sidestep past her.

'Matt was just a kid when I left. I need to know what kind of man he's grown into. Is he a troublemaker, or did I just see him reach his limit today? Where does he stand in all this?'

'He's a fine young man. Where he stands is difficult to say now Bill and May are gone.'

He shrugged as though the silence would answer for him. Instead, his reluctance to give her the details infuriated her, coming on top of everything else.

'You might as well come out with it. What about Matt? I still know you well enough to recognize when you're not telling me something you think might upset me.'

A half-hearted chuckle confirmed her fears. 'Matt's close as a brother to me. Him and Ava come over to dinner once a month and we talk. Before the killing started, I'd say Matt was the most likely to give Swain what he wanted.'

'The Circle Double L? You've got to be joking,' she scoffed.

'Bill and Maybelle lived for that ranch and what it stands for, but Matt takes after you. He's got other dreams, other priorities, especially now.'

'Priorities? Such as?' she asked, trying to keep impatience from her tone. 'And who's Ava?'

Tom's eyes twinkled with mischief. 'I think he

should be the one to bring you up to date, but you'll like Ava. As for Matt, he's a good kid. He's a lot like you.' He hesitated. 'A lot like Emmett too.'

A wall of silence descended between them.

'You promised you'd never mention that,' she said after a lengthy pause. 'My pa never admitted Emmett was his son.'

He'd never denied it either, just said there was no proof. Of course, Emmett had told a different story when she caught up with him, and the thousand dollar bank draft he had in her father's name. . . .

'There was no proof. None,' she said, choosing to forget the rest.

Tom nodded. 'Well, you might want to consider it. I think that possibility is the only thing that's been keeping Matt alive. Emmett doesn't seem to have any stomach for killing the only person in the West family who's treated him like anything other than a cur.'

'That's not true. I left my family to look for him. I sacrificed everything.' Her voice cracked. 'Look, I don't want to talk about the past. Matt brought me back here for a reason and I'm not going to over-think it. I just want to go home. Be a family again.'

CHAPTER 9

Standing in the sheriff's office, Jake poured himself coffee. It was lukewarm and weak and he shuddered as he gulped it down.

'You look a mite upset, Jake,' Riley observed.

'I guess you could say that.' Jake didn't trust himself to elaborate.

'Can't say I blame you. I'm not sure how I feel about that whole situation myself.'

Jake's illusions dissolved, although he couldn't bring himself to ask the obvious. Instead, he waited, cup touching his lips, eyes narrowed, his frayed temper ready to go either way.

'She's quite a woman, Matt's sister. Phewee. Imagine a little lady like that challenging Radley to a gunfight. That's something to tell your grandkids about.' He wagged a twisted finger at Jake. 'Put you in the middle of a bad situation though, didn't she?'

Despair at the sheriff's near-sightedness rendered Jake speechless. First, there was a crazy, gun-toting woman. Now, he had to contend with an old friend who, for some unknown reason, had brought him face to face with a dangerous past and probably couldn't find his own backside with both hands. He hadn't thought his disbelief could sink any lower, but it had, and he almost dropped his cup before he could return it to the stove.

Taking a minute to compose himself, he swallowed the bitter aftertaste of coffee, determined not to let Riley's ignorance continue. 'Actually, Riley, I wasn't thinking about her. To tell the truth, I'm more riled by what you've done than what she did.'

Riley stopped smiling. 'Me? What have I done?'

'Well, I was kinda hopin' to keep the fact that I'm a marshal to myself, take a quiet look around and maybe find out what's going on from the inside. You pretty much blew that idea sky high.'

'I didn't have much choice after your lady-friend started making threats.'

'Nice try, Riley, but she doesn't know who I am or who I was before, remember? My secret's safe with her. Swain's the one who worries me, nearly as much as you do.'

Colour flooded Riley's already ruddy cheeks. 'Now, wait a minute, what's that supposed to mean?'

'You preached to me about the past not always being a good place to revisit and then you pitch me face to face with the first man I ever sent to prison.'

'What?' Riley seemed genuinely surprised.

'Don't you know who Emmett Swain is, or should I say, was?'

'Some fella who had a falling out with a man in town a few years ago and left to make his fortune is all I heard.'

'Let me put it into some kind of order for you. Jay Langerud – Parley Jones – and Emmett Swain, who you'd probably know by his alias, Jim West.'

'Jim West! You mean Swain is. . . ?'

Jake nodded. 'That's right. The man who nearly, but apparently not quite, paid the price for Jay Langerud's new life as Jake Rudd, lawman.'

'Well, isn't that a coincidence, him calling himself West and now he's hell bent on destroying a family with that name.' The sheriff paled as quickly as he coloured up. 'Jake, boy, I'm sorry. I didn't know, I swear. I thought West was still locked up.' He sighed. 'Do you think he busted out?'

'I haven't heard anything about it if he did. Probably got himself a good attorney. The judge said at the time my written testimony wasn't much to put him away with, considering my own past.'

Riley pondered a moment. 'Kind of changes things a bit though, don't it? A man who knows Swain, how he thinks, could be mighty useful to this town. I knew if anybody could straighten this mess out, you'd be the man. You're tough but fair, you shoot from the hip and—'

Jake held up his hand, silencing the sheriff before his own infamy made him feel physically sick coming so close on the back of the bad coffee. 'It's a good story. You've done a lot to improve it over the years,' he said, drily. 'The plain fact is, I'm nothing but a man with a price on his head now. I wrote and resigned as a US marshal more 'n a month ago.'

'You did what? You're the best lawman in these parts.'

Jake gave a non-committal shrug, uncomfortable with the details of his own reputation. When the chips were down, he did what he had to. Anything else was hearsay and make-believe. But as the sheriff concentrated on toying with a pencil stub, Jake decided there was no point trying to enlighten him.

For a few seconds, neither of them said a word. The silence seemed to bother Riley more than it did Jake and finally, after a lot of huffing and puffing, he exploded.

'Well, whether you're official or not, you're in this with the rest of us now.' He pushed back in his chair, balancing precariously before he kicked his legs up onto the desk. 'Yes, sir, you're here for the duration, like it or not. If Swain does recognize you, there's nowhere you'll be able to go without looking over your shoulder twenty-four hours a day.'

'I disappeared once before.'

'Mmm, maybe, but I've got a feeling. . . .'

Jake braced himself, sure a pause could only mean trouble. 'You might as well come out with it,' he said, after a few seconds of waiting to find out what new calamity awaited him.

'Well . . .' Another infuriating hesitation followed. 'I'm retiring next week. Found myself a friendly widow and decided to settle down to a quiet life. Nobody else wants this job. That'll pretty much make you the only law around here.'

A hammer blow couldn't have hit Jake any harder. The last thing he wanted was to get caught up, maybe even killed, when he was so close to folding his hand.

71

A dozen violent scenarios filled his mind, from wringing the sheriff's neck to shooting him dead. Only their long friendship kept his hands pinned at his sides.

Finally, he unclenched his jaw enough to speak. 'Why didn't you just come straight out and tell me that's what you were up to?'

'I'm sorry, Jake. You promised me five years and that's what you've given me, but I hoped you'd change your mind about quitting. I heard about your resignation, but this town needs somebody like you. I'm no match for the mercenaries Swain's hiring, especially if he's who you say he is. Bill West tried standing up to them and he got a bullet in his back. Young Matt's a good k—' He almost fell off his chair when Jake strode to the door. 'Hey, where are you going?'

'To the hotel.'

'What for?'

Jake sucked in a steadying breath. 'I'm tired. I'm hungry. And now I'm facing trouble I thought I buried three years ago.'

'You can't leave yet. We need to talk, make a plan.'

Jake turned and glared at him. 'You really don't want to be talking to me right now. Not if you want to believe all those good things you made up about me.'

The sheriff's chair landed with a thud, but the sheriff made no move to get up. He stared at Jake, shaking his head as if he'd lost a dollar and found a dime.

'Jake, maybe I made a mistake, but there's been a lot of blood spilt in this town and there'll be a lot more before this business is finished. These folks need you. That boy and his sister need you. Just sleep on it, will you? If you ain't changed your mind by mornin', I'll buy you a ticket on the next train and I'll never mention this again.' He paused. 'What do you say?'

Jake wanted to say the sheriff was a damn fool, but he didn't like to insult a friend. He forced a stiff nod then strode into the street, taking a deep breath of cool afternoon air before he started walking. He'd barely taken ten paces before he heard himself being hailed.

'Howdy, Marshal.'

Unexpectedly, the childish voice calmed his temper and his smile was genuine when he looked down at Jimmy McKendrick. The boy's face shone with excitement as he trailed Jake towards the hotel.

'I heard what happened. When are you goin' to arrest Swain?' he asked, his voice rising to a hysterical pitch.

Jimmy's certainty soured Jake's mood, but he tried not to let it show. After all, the boy's assumption wasn't surprising. 'Not today, Jimmy. He didn't do anything.'

'Didn't do anything?' Jimmy gripped Jake's wrist, his feet leaving the ground as he used all his weight to tug him to a stop. 'He killed Mrs West. You were there. You have to arrest him. You have to—'

'I'm sorry, Jimmy, I didn't see him shoot anybody. The lady shot him.'

'But . . .' He seemed on the verge of tears, his fists pounding Jake's thigh as lack of comprehension stalled his argument.

Gripping the boy's shoulder, Jake held him at arm's length. When Jimmy finally quieted, Jake softened his

tone and tried reasoning with him. 'Surely you understand I can't arrest somebody for getting shot.' He
didn't add that he'd like to. Swain might not have
pulled the trigger, but he was paying the man who had,
and in Jake's book that amounted to the same thing.
'Jimmy, I'm sorry.'

'Sorry don't bring my pa back. Sorry don't bring
Mrs West back,' Jimmy shot back quick as a .45.
Although his anger had subsided, the boy's sullen
expression hid none of his resentment and he
sounded surprisingly wise for his tender years. 'My ma
always told me a man don't need to say sorry as long as
he's doing the best he can.'

Damn! The boy aimed high and his words were right
on target. Nothing the sheriff had said had touched
Jake's conscience, but seeing the disappointment
etched on Jimmy's face was like a bullet slicing
between Jake's ribs. It had the power to humble him,
but stubbornly, he refused to let it sway his decision.

Jake chose the easy way out and changed the
subject. 'Did you get yourself something good to eat
the way I told you?'

Jimmy frowned. 'I had all on to prove to Miss Peggy
at the café that I didn't steal the money. When I told
her it was you that gave it me, she said she was going to
get you to lock me in jail if I was lying.'

It wasn't a real answer, but Jake couldn't help chuckling at the speed Jimmy's priorities had shifted and he
didn't give him a chance to backtrack. 'Don't worry, I'll
straighten her out. Where are you off to now?'

Hanging his head, Jimmy shrugged, the perfect

picture of dejection. 'Don't know. Thought maybe I could tag along with you for a while. I could really help, be a lookout or somethin'.'

Unease tickled the back of Jake's neck. He liked Jimmy, but whether or not he decided to stay in Langley, there was no place in his life for a ten-year-old boy. The problem was how he could explain that in the face of unshakeable childish optimism.

Footsteps approaching and a familiar voice offered a temporary reprieve.

'Don't let him fool you, Marshal. He's not as hard done by as he looks.'

Jake looked up to see Matt striding towards them. 'It's good to see you again.'

'I guessed you could do with rescuing.' Matt faked a swipe to Jimmy's ear, an action that earned him a grin that oozed admiration and cleverly shifted the boy's attention away from Jake. 'Mrs Mallen at the bakery told me to send you right over there if I saw you, Jimmy. She was baking apple pies when I left. They smelt real good.'

Jimmy dodged Matt's second attempt to ruffle his hair. 'But me and the marshal was just going to—'

'Oh, that can wait. Sounds as though you should run on over there,' Jake said, winking at Matt.

'But what about Swain?'

'Don't worry, Jimmy. Bad men always get what's coming to them.' Jake gave him a gentle shove. 'Now, go.'

Jimmy stood his ground, but his interest in Jake had waned, and gripping Matt's sleeve, he asked, 'Can I come out to the Circle Double L yet and work for you?'

'I told you, as soon as me and Mr Swain sort out our differences. Until then, you stay here and keep out of trouble. All right, Jimmy?'

Jimmy nodded, but his slumped shoulders showed he was far from happy with the arrangement when he walked away. Jake watched him go, waiting until he was out of earshot before he turned to Matt.

'He seems like a good kid.'

'He is. I'd take him with me now if I thought he'd be safe.'

Jake resisted the urge to ask for clarification. He already had too much information to be impartial. 'How's your sister.'

'I don't know. I left her at Doc Bailey's. They're old friends. If anyone can talk some sense into her, he can.' Matt extended his hand. 'I don't think we've been introduced. I'm Matthew West. Most folks just call me Matt.'

Jake liked a man who wasn't afraid to make the first move, and he could tell a lot from a handshake. He held it just long enough to take the measure of the young man who so far had impressed him with his level-headedness. Again, he liked what he found. The kid had a positive grip with just the right amount of confidence.

'I have been introduced thanks to the sheriff. Jake or Rudd will do just fine, whichever suits you.'

Their stares locked and Jake realized he wasn't the only one making a judgement.

'Well, it's been a long day, Marshal, I better get going.'

'Give your sister my regards. Maybe you could tell her I need to talk with her when she's feeling up to it.'

Matt frowned. 'You're not going to arrest her, are you?'

Jake almost laughed until he realized the kid was serious. 'No. It's personal.'

It was easy to read an honest man, and Matt was an honest man, Jake decided, as he watched his reaction. First, there was relief. Next, there was a slight frown and a narrowing of the eyes. Finally, there was the deliberate look of indifference.

'We're going back to the ranch. I can't speak for Ros but I don't imagine she'll be coming back to town anytime soon. She never did like Langley after what happened.' The last remark was more of a mumbled aside, a slip of the tongue. His attempt to cover it was loud and clumsy. 'You're welcome to ride out to the L. It wouldn't hurt for you to see what all the fighting's about.'

An awkward silence separated them as a dozen questions filled Jake's head. There was no doubt in his mind that he would accept the invitation. It wouldn't have made any difference whether he had one or not, but what he really wanted to know was more about Ros's brother. The bond between the pair was clearly strong, if awkward. So why hadn't Jake ever heard about him? And what about the rest of the family?

'Maybe I'll do that,' he said, coolly.

'You should. My wife enjoys company.' Matt touched the brim of his Derby and continued into the hotel.

Jake watched him leave, noting his easy gait and the

quiet confidence that contradicted his youthfulness. And a wife? That was a surprise. The more he saw of him, the more he liked Ros's brother, and the easier it became to take sides. As he continued to the hotel, Jake couldn't help wondering what kind of handshake Emmett Swain would have after all this time.

CHAPTER 10

After a satisfactory meal in the hotel dining room, a cigar at the bar, and a whiskey he didn't touch, Jake said good night early. Back in his room, he sat on the narrow bed and removed his boots before lying down. Sleeping in his clothes was a habit, something he did when he wasn't sure what his next move would be. Tonight, that realization bothered him more than usual.

With his hat tipped across his eyes, he wedged his elbow behind his head and tried to relax. It only took a minute for the spent mattress to convince him he was on a road to nowhere. Even worse, although sleep weighed heavy on his body, his mind refused to let go of recent events. He'd already replayed each of them at least a dozen times throughout the night, weighing every detail. Still he hadn't reached a conclusion and it annoyed the hell out of him.

Why was he making it so hard on himself when he already knew the answer? When he saw Ros pop out of the crowd, he'd known this was where he belonged. The only thing wrong with this particular scenario was an old enemy with a band of mercenaries, a ten-year-old boy looking for revenge, and the lady in question trying her damnedest to get killed. Not to mention Matt, who deserved help just because he didn't ask for any.

Hell, a man could go insane! But right now, he didn't have time with someone banging on his door hard enough to loosen the panels.

'Mr Rudd. Marshal, let me in.'

Jimmy?

Jake pushed his hat away from his face and slid his gun into its holster.

'Please. Hurry. Marshal, let me in.'

Out of habit, Jake kicked his feet into his boots before unlocking the door. He barely had time to open it before Jimmy flew into his arms.

'They're coming for you, Marshal,' he blurted out. 'They're coming to kill you.'

'Easy, Jimmy. Who? Who's coming?'

Jimmy gulped, trying to speak as he struggled to catch his breath. 'I heard them. They're coming for you and the lady.'

'Who, Jimmy? Slow down and tell—'

Glass shattered, a volley of bullets thudding into the wall opposite the window as Jake dived for cover. He shielded Jimmy with his body, waiting a few seconds after the shots stopped before crawling to the sill and peeking out. Nothing but darkness greeted him. He was starting to hate this room.

'Jimmy, I want you to go home. Don't come near me again. It's not safe.'

As he turned, his toe slipped in a pool of blood, bringing him to his knees on the floor where Jimmy lay face down, unconscious, at least Jake hoped he was as he checked his wrist for a pulse. With his own heart-beat racing, it was difficult to find the boy's, and when he did, it was weak. He turned him over, close to panic at the sight of a gash that started near his right eye, streaked across his temple and then nicked the top of his ear.

'Jimmy can you hear me.'

He sensed movement behind him in the hallway. 'Are you all right, Marshal?' It was a woman he'd seen in the restaurant.

Jake folded Jimmy's twisted arm across his chest then cradled his head in the crook of his elbow as he lifted his limp body. 'Where's the doc's office?'

The woman's mouth moved but no sound came out as she clutched her collar to her throat. Impatiently, Jake pushed past her and bolted down the stairs two at a time. As he reached the last step, a door off the lower hallway opened and a man emerged tucking in his shirt-tails as he careered into the light.

'Matt? I thought you left hours ago.'

'Doc wanted Ros to rest up a while, so we decided to stay.' Matt turned slightly, wrapping his arm around the woman who waddled out beside him. 'This is my wife, Ava. Ava, this is Marshal Rudd.'

She was at least a head shorter than Matt, sunshine pretty, and almost as round as she was tall. Beneath a mass of blonde hair that cascaded to her waist, her pregnancy preceded her as she shuffled to meet Jake.

He glimpsed large blue eyes before she fixed her attention on Jimmy.

'What happened?'

'He came to warn me, got caught up in the cross-fire.' He looked over Ava's head as a new thought occurred to him. 'Matt, where's your sister?'

Ros woke with a start, unnerved by the sound of distant gunshots. Overhead, floorboards creaked as Tom left his bed, and getting stiffly out of her chair in the surgery, Ros stumbled through the darkness to meet him.

Before she reached the hallway, heavy footfalls thundered down the stairs and in a couple of long strides, a red-haired man she didn't recognize closed in on her. She reached for her gun too late as he punched out, knocking her backwards and sending the weapon skittering through the darkness. Scurrying backwards, she tried to avoid his hand, but he was too quick and dragged her up and off the floor in a frenzy of kicking and cursing.

Adjusting his grip to her throat, he shook her hard. 'Settle down, lady. I didn't come to kill you but don't think I ain't up for the idea.'

His fingers dug into her windpipe and she gave up the fight, knowing she couldn't win.

'Not so tough now are you, little lady?' he whispered against her ear. 'It must have felt really good standing up to Radley, all the while knowing the marshal was there to back you up. I heard you and him were quite a handful. You remember Shorty and Barclay and

Sulley, don't you?'

He dropped her and she stumbled, rubbing her neck. 'What do you want?'

'I want to kill you, the way you killed Shorty with a bullet in the gut, but I'm not going to just yet.' He grabbed a handful of her shirt and yanked her towards the door. 'Mr Swain's got some business he wants to discuss with you first, but when he's finished, you're all mine.'

Panic fortified her with the strength to lash out. He hadn't been expecting it and she broke away, careering along the hallway before he caught her and flung her against the wall.

'You won't get away with this.'

'Who's going to stop me? The marshal?' He laughed, back-handing her around the head. 'You heard the gunshots, didn't you?'

'The door's been forced,' Matt said, pushing the broken lock into place. 'Ros!'

'Matt, wait!'

Jake followed with the boy cradled in his arms and Ava jostling for a position at his elbow. Luckily, it was Tom who stumbled down the stairs to meet them. He leaned against the stair-rail mopping his brow as he peered at Jimmy. The boy's complexion contrasted sharply with the blood plastered in his hair and the developing bruise accentuating a lump on his fore-head the size of an egg. He didn't move or make a sound to show he was alive.

'Bring him in and lay him on the table,' the doc

said, shoving past Ava who was already lighting a lamp. 'Let me get a look at him.'

Jake placed Jimmy in the treatment room. Tom staggered as he leaned over, patting his brow one last time before throwing down the towel and making a close inspection of Jimmy's visible wounds.

'Where's Ros?' Matt asked.

'Clay Carson took her.'

'Are you sure?'

'Yep. He woke me up and made sure I knew it was him before he knocked me out.'

Matt started for the door, but Jake intercepted him. 'Where are you going?'

'The Crystal Slipper. Carson works for Swain so you can bet that's where he's taken her.'

Rudd shuffled a couple of inches, but his fingers remained locked on Matt's forearm. 'Just wait a minute.' His gaze spun to the doc and Ava. 'Is Jimmy gonna be all right, Doc?'

'It's difficult to say. Any wound to the head is serious,' the doc said, methodically cleaning the blood away. 'There's no blood in his ears so I have to assume there are no fractures. I need to take a good look at him, but we can hope.'

'Good, but before you do anything else, you need to barricade the door.'

The doc looked up, obviously confused.

'Whatever happens, I don't want you to let anyone in, and if anybody comes asking about the boy, don't tell them a thing.' He headed out.

'Matt,' Ava said quietly, as she methodically rolled

up her sleeves.

The kid was already moving towards the hallway, but he stopped on a dime. She met his worried look with a steady, confident one of her own.

'Be careful.'

Matt let out his breath. 'Tom, do you still have that old shotgun?'

'It's by the front door.'

Matt collected it on the way out. 'Marshal, wait up!'

Jake half turned as he strode purposefully towards the saloon. 'You know this is a bad idea, don't you, kid?'

Matt fell in beside him. 'What choice do we have?'

Jake stopped beneath a lantern, no doubt hung out to guide a wayward husband home. Facing Matt in the flickering yellow haze, he looked him in the eye.

'Tell me, Matt, do you think marching into the Crystal Slipper is the right way to do this?'

'Hell if I know.'

Jake was impressed with the kid's honesty. It was the kind of answer he'd expected.

'So why are we?'

A sigh plumed white in the air. 'My sister's in there for one and I'm not about to sit around while Swain and his band of mercenaries do God-only-knows what to her.' Matt clasped the shotgun in both hands, raising it between him and Jake. 'This has been the law here for a while now. I think you knew that well before Jimmy got shot. I'm not saying it's right, but that's how it is.'

Jake couldn't resist a question that had been bothering him. 'I saw what happened today with you, Swain and Radley. Your sister thought you wanted to get yourself killed, but you didn't, did you? Even with your sister-in-law's body still warm on the ground, you somehow wanted to put a peaceable end to . . . whatever it is that's causing this poison to spread.'

'You're a fancy talker, Marshal. I could almost believe you, but, to be honest, I'm not sure how far I would've gone – how far I will go.' He scuffed his toe in the dirt. 'I've tried to find some middle ground with Swain, even after my brother Bill was killed, but . . . I dunno. I'm starting to believe this is the only way to reason with him.'

There was no malice, just plainly stated fact.

'We could just turn around and go back, fetch some reinforcements,' Jake suggested, testing the kid's resolve.

Matt's knuckles whitened around the shotgun. 'I'll be honest with you. I'm scared to death of what's going to happen when we walk in there, and I don't really know where you stand in all this, but I'm prepared to go on a little faith and say it's your call.'

An old, familiar gut instinct kicked in. It had been a long time since Jake had considered deliberately lighting a fuse under trouble. He liked to think age and experience had slowed him down, but maybe it was just lack of incentive. That wasn't going to be a problem now. Not when an innocent ten-year-old boy was fighting for his life, a woman was missing, and the man probably responsible was undoubtedly drinking to his own success.

'We both know we should turn around, walk away and wait for Swain to make the next move; I wouldn't blame you if you did. After all, you've got a wife to consider and a baby on the way.'

Matt's shrug was non-committal and unconvincing and Jake held out his hand, waiting until Matt took it in a firm grip.

'All right then. Let's take a walk.'

CHAPTER 11

Ros spluttered as cold water splashed her face. 'I'm awake. There's no need to try and drown me.'

Somewhere nearby, music and laughter mingled in a raucous din, punctuated by the clink of glasses and the rumble of voices. Opening her eyes, she blinked several times against the brightness cast by a lamp held close to her face. Behind it, two men watched her, their features blurred by the glare.

She forced herself awkwardly into a sitting position.

'Is this business or pleasure?' she asked, finding herself wallowing on a soft mattress in a room garishly decorated and perfumed to high heaven.

'Shut up and listen.'

Her hand came up automatically to block the slap that followed.

'Carson, if you touch her again, you're finished in this town.'

She recognized Emmett's lazy tone, and the man who had kidnapped her from the doc's house. He grunted and stepped back into the shadows. Left to his own means, he would undoubtedly take pleasure in doling out more than a slap.

'What do you want?' Ros asked, fighting the urge to make a move for the door, too eager to find out her fate.

Emmett swaggered towards her, stopping within inches to stare down at her. He had changed into a black suit since she'd last seen him and his complexion contrasted pale as milk against it. His dark eyes shone black as coal, making her think of his heart.

'Don't worry. I'm not going to kill you just yet. I only want to clear up a few things before you think about settling back in Langley.'

It was on the tip of her tongue to admit she had no intention of staying more than a day or two, but mischief got the better of her. As a child, she'd always enjoyed teasing Emmett. An orphan passed from family to family, he'd been eager to fit in, an easy target for harmless pranks. Maybe it was her guilt, and not love, that had finally brought them together then torn them apart. She'd certainly paid a high price for her part in his downfall.

She stiffened her back and raised her chin defiantly. 'I came home to see my family.' The reference made her wince as she waited for a reaction, but there wasn't one. 'I'm willing to include you in that group, Emmett, whatever you might think. Let the past lie.'

'It's not that simple. You cost me three years of my life. You and your lover. You should have stayed dead – both of you. At the very least, you shouldn't have shown your faces here.'

His rambling made no sense. He'd always been able

to put two-and-two together and come up with five. The coincidence of her arriving in town at the same time as Rudd would be enough for Emmett's imagination to conjure a hundred twisted scenarios. But why blame her for costing him three years of his life?

'So the only thing standing between you and the L would have been Matt?' she asked, cutting to the chase.

'After all this time, you still think you know everything.'

'I know you're still holding a grudge. You should let it go. What happened was wrong, but it's in the past.'

He grinned, revealing tobacco stained teeth. 'Still trying to make everything right after all this time? Well, sweet as that is, me, I take betrayal seriously.' His laughter filled the room, crushing her under the weight of its irony. 'Don't think your exile is payment enough for what you did to me. I wanted you dead and that hasn't changed. You've been living on borrowed time and I intend to take it back when you've seen me destroy what's left of the West name and fortune.'

She forced herself not to strike out and give him the satisfaction of knowing just how much his words affected her, but her tongue wouldn't stay still.

'I forfeited three years of my life trying to make up for what happened to you. Isn't that enough?'

'I have to admit, it turned out better than I imagined. I thought you being dead would be enough, but I feel so much more fulfilled, knowing you've suffered.' He nodded with a smug grin. 'You should use that hatred I see in your eyes, but don't let it blind you to the simple truth that I will get what I want.'

His certainty irritated her. 'What do you want? My father's dead. Bill and May. Matt was too young to know what was going on and me . . . I loved you. I know you never doubted that. Didn't I turn my back on my family, follow you across Kansas and. . . .' She couldn't say more as her missing memories plunged her into a pit of nothingness.

'So let's all pretend we're one happy family?' Emmett laughed. 'Nice try, Ros, but after what happened, my hatred runs too deep for that. You're dead to me.'

Carson stepped forward, rubbing his palms together excitedly. 'Can I have her now, boss?'

'Shut up.' Emmett gave Ros a crooked smile. 'I'll tell you when.'

'But what about Shorty and Sully and Barclay? She—'

Emmett backhanded the big man, drawing blood from a split lip. 'I said, shut up. In fact, get out of here.'

He waited for the door to close behind Carson and his mumbled curses to fade. Then, after a slight pause, he dropped to his haunches and took Ros's hand in his own. She tried to pull away, but he held tight, crushing her fingers until she relaxed.

'Have you told Matt the truth yet? Told him that I'm the oldest brother and the ranch is already mine.'

'You're the bastard brother, with no proof to say otherwise. You've got no claim.'

He grinned. 'Surely you remember Pa's letter.'

Ros's mind worked into a frenzy of denial but if he still had the letter. . . .

'Doesn't Matt deserve to know what this is all about? You ran away; doesn't he deserve the same chance?'

'He won't run,' she said, bitterly.

Emmett shrugged. 'What other choice does he have? I own most of this town and most of the people in it. I don't have to spell it out for you, do I?'

A lifeline swung to the fore of Ros's confusion. 'Aren't you forgetting somebody?'

'Your friend the marshal? Or should I say Jay Langerud?'

His nails dug into her skin until she thought her bones must snap. Ros's nerve faltered as a long-forgotten image flashed through her mind.

'You look surprised, Ros. That was an unfortunate mistake you made earlier, letting me see you together and reminding me of the last time I saw you both. I have to admit I was surprised. He's got more forgiveness in his soul than I have.' He stroked her cheek. 'If you'd put a bullet in my back. . . .'

She stared at him, her mind as blank as a new notebook.

'Of course, it worked out well for me. Who wouldn't believe that in your grief you threw yourself under those horses?'

Realization exploded like a stopper from a bottle. Emmett, or someone he had paid, had pushed her in front of that stage. Undoubtedly, Emmett had been the one paying the most recent bounty on her. What Jake's role in the whole affair had been, she didn't know but the need to defend him raged inside her.

'I wouldn't underestimate him.'

'I don't intend to, but despite what he did to me, he's not really my concern. You see, when I tell Radley that the man who killed Parley Jones – his pa – is in town, I think that particular problem's going to take care of itself.

'In the meantime, talk to Matt.' He stood abruptly, shoving her so she sprawled on the bed. 'He's a good kid. I don't know why I should like him but I do. Still, if things get dirty, you know me, I always enjoy a fight and I don't let people or sentiment stand in my way. You and Jay are dead already, but Matt. . . .'

Ros made a grab for him as he turned to leave, but missed and lay back on the bed, staring at the boarded ceiling as the door opened and closed. There'd be other times to fight. Right now, she needed to think of a way out of this mess.

CHAPTER 12

A dozen loafers and whores cluttered the Crystal Slipper when Jake and Matt arrived. Jake surveyed the interior through a window before pushing between the batwing doors. His breath caught as he entered. He never got used to the stench of sawdust and spilt whiskey mingling with cheap perfume and sweat. It took a second for his eyes to adjust to the haze of smoke hovering in the low-lit room.

Stiff backs and mumbled conversations greeted him as he weaved his way between tables. As he neared the long maple bar, a saggy old whore started towards him, half-dressed and startlingly garish with painted eyebrows and vivid red lips.

'Buy me a drink, mister?'

Jake sidestepped and leaned his elbows on the bar. His gaze rested on the mirrored reflections of Radley, Swain, and a bull-sized, redheaded man he didn't recognize. They'd been playing cards, but now the game seemed to have lost its interest as they watched him.

The whore moved in closer, the stench of sex

preceding her. 'Did you hear me, mister? I said, buy me a drink?'

'Flo, you leave Mr Rudd alone,' Swain shouted. 'He looks a mite upset. Better make that whiskey a double, Frank, on the house.'

The same bartender who had served Jake earlier pushed forward a glass and filled it. Then he stood back, running his fingers through his thinning hair while he waited.

Jake's gaze flicked to the liquor then back to his quarry. Strange he should think of them that way, but the tension buzzing around him added an element of sport to the situation. Deliberately, he slammed a coin on the polished bar and saw Frank leap into the air.

'I'll pay for my own drink, if it's all the same to you.' He tipped his head back to drink, just enough that he didn't lose sight of Swain.

A lull descended over the room, the silence broken only by the discreet movement of a chair scraped across dry boards. Frank's eyes rolled as he looked nervously between the money and his boss.

Swain straightened in his seat looking uncomfortable despite his ever-present smirk. His skin shone pale and sweaty against the severity of his black shirt and suit. The only glimpse of colour was a red sling, half-hidden beneath his coat, and supporting his injured arm. His redundant sleeve disappeared inside its armhole giving him a lopsided, comical appearance.

'Just trying to be friendly, Mr Rudd. Interest you in a hand of cards maybe?'

Jake turned through ninety degrees, holding his

drink in his left hand, he swallowed it and slipped the glass back onto the bar. 'I think, maybe before we go any further, there's something you should know about me, Mr Swain.'

'And what would that be, Mr Rudd? That you took a look around and decided this ain't your kinda town?'

Jake rankled at Swain's disdain, but he pretended to consider the idea as a dozen snickers circled the room. 'You need to know that I don't play games.'

Swain looked first at Radley, then the redhead, before returning his attention to Jake. 'I'm not sure I follow.'

'Well, say for instance a man comes after me with a gun, he better be ready to face me.' Jake's glare lingered on the redhead sitting to Swain's left and easing his neck inside his collar like a turkey. 'Not shoot into the dark like a yellow-bellied coward.'

The big man shifted in his chair, his mouth drawing into a grim line. Jake tensed, his senses screaming. Was this what he'd come looking for? A fight? What the hell had he been thinking? That he could reason with men who would kidnap and murder women and children? A stark image of Jimmy, small and twisted, lying in a pool of blood, crossed his mind. That's what he'd been thinking about when he walked into the Crystal Slipper.

As quickly as his doubts surfaced, they disappeared. 'You got something to say, big man?' he asked the redhead.

Jake caught sight of a small movement as Frank shuffled closer to the bar. To Swain's right, Radley sat stock-still, three cards fanned out in his left hand, his right hand resting on his outstretched thigh. A telltale fever glistened in his eyes.

Everyone else in the room seemed frozen. Out of the corner of his eye, Jake reassessed them. Mostly, they appeared to be worn-out whores and broken down men, there because they had nowhere else to go. When the shooting started, he was sure they'd hold fire until a winner started to emerge.

With renewed calm, Jake addressed Swain. 'I guess you heard what happened. Twice today I've been shot at. I didn't come over here looking for the culprit. I just came to set a few things straight, since I know a saloon is a good place to start a rumour.'

Swain leaned back in his chair and pulled out a cheroot. With the arrogance only a man who knows his back is covered can have, he shifted his sights to Radley, waiting until the gunman struck a match and lit his smoke. After a few gentle puffs, he returned his attention to Jake.

'Well, Mr Rudd, you're probably right about that. So, what happens now?' He smiled around the room, fuelling the oppressive atmosphere. 'Do we each take a guess, or are you gonna say what's on your mind?'

'First, I want you,' he inclined his chin in Frank's direction, keeping his main focus on Radley and Swain, 'to move away from that rifle, or whatever it is you're hiding under there, and put your hands flat on the bar.'

Frank feigned innocence with a shrug. 'I don't know what you mean.'

'I think you do, Frank Hardy,' Matt called out.

He had slipped in through the batwing doors, the shotgun aimed at the bartender. With a slight nod to Jake, he pressed his back to the wall and fanned the barrel around the room. Jake released his breath. He hadn't exactly doubted Matt, but he'd taken a risk trusting a kid to watch his back. Slowly and precisely, he unfastened his jacket and dipped his fingers into his waistcoat pocket. Striding towards Swain's table, he pulled out a US marshal's badge.

'Do you see this?' Jake asked, carefully pinning it to his left lapel. 'This badge means that when you speak to me, you call me Marshal or Marshal Rudd, not Mr Rudd. Do you understand?'

Swain gave the briefest of nods.

Carson wiped his mouth with the back of his hand and laughed. 'A piece o' shit is still a piece o' shit. Don't matter what name you give it.'

He didn't see Jake's elbow before it smashed into his face. There wasn't time as his chair upended and he spewed backwards onto the floor. Rolling in the spit and sawdust, it was obviously all he could do to breathe as he clutched his twisted nose and tried not to choke on his own blood.

'Je-sus, Ru— Marshal,' Swain corrected quickly as he dived right, knocking Radley half to the floor and clinging to his own injured arm as if it were detached.

Jake's gun appeared in his hand, covering Radley before the shootist could reach for his. He looked directly at Radley, who paused half-crouched, his hands fanned out at arm's length. Spilt whiskey stained his tan leather waistcoat and the front of his shirt. With his hair mussed and a snarl curling his lips, he didn't look half as confident as he had a moment before.

Jake waited for Radley to relax, then scanned the whole room. 'Now all of you understand this. I'm a United States Marshal, bound to uphold the law, and I take my responsibility very seriously. An innocent boy was shot tonight and a woman was kidnapped. At least one of you knows where she is, and I want to know what you know.'

Radley's fingers flexed, but his hand stayed clear of his holster.

Swain picked himself up from his position sprawled across the card table. 'Now what makes you think we know anything about a kidnapping, Marshal?'

Jake hauled Carson to his knees. 'Because this,' he said, pulling several strands of long hair off Carson's shirtfront, 'is a pretty close match for—'

'Don't waste your time, Marshal. I'm here.'

Ros materialized from the shadows at the back of the saloon and strode directly to Jake. Standing between him and his adversaries, she looked pale and unsteady, but her chin was raised at a defiant angle. He cut his eyes at the fresh bruises appearing on her face, feeling anger burn in the pit of his stomach.

'Which one of them took you?'

She shook her head and started past him, hesitating when he didn't immediately follow. This time she spoke in barely more than a whisper.

'If you don't want to die tonight, it's your turn to trust me. There's a man up on the balcony, and another lurking behind the piano. You don't stand a chance. Just back up and let's get out of here while we still can.'

Behind her, Swain nodded his agreement. 'You said what you came here to say, Marshal, and you saved the girl. No reason to try your luck any more tonight.'

Jake's arm stiffened, the gun in his hand rising slightly as he refreshed his aim. Swain was too cocky, but before he could bring him down a peg, Ros fainted against him. He had little choice other than to catch her.

Laughter pealed around the room. As he struggled to hold Ros and keep his weapon steady, Jake noticed even Radley had a gleam of amusement melting the ice behind his eyes.

Swain straightened his chair and picked up his cards. 'Looks as if your responsibilities might just have changed, Marshal.' He shuffled and dealt hands to Radley and Carson. 'Anything else?'

Things hadn't quite gone as Jake anticipated, but for now it looked as though his best decision would be to cut and run. Placing his trust in Matt, he slid his gun back in its holster and swung Ros up into his arms, then he backed out of the saloon and melted into the night.

CHAPTER 13

In a room at the back of the doc's house, a lamp flickered on a dresser and a stove pressed into the corner had been banked and lit. Although it popped and cracked, its warmth was slow in penetrating the bitter cold. When they entered, Tom glanced up from slipping Jimmy into the narrow bed then made another check of the thick bandages around the boy's head and arm.

'How is he, Doc?' Rudd asked softly.

Ros threw herself into the only chair in the room, watching Jake's expression change from business to concern as his gaze fastened on the boy.

'The bullet came as close to killing him as I'd ever want to see,' Tom said, rolling down his shirtsleeve. 'As far as I can tell, it skimmed his skull but there are no fractures. His arm's broken. I've splinted it and it should heal well enough. I'd say it's a miracle he's alive at all.'

'So he'll be all right?' Rudd asked, optimism bringing the power back into his voice as he approached the bed and touched the bandages.

'He should regain consciousness within the next twenty-four hours. We won't know until then.'

Rudd offered a handshake. 'Thanks for what you've done, Doc. Don't worry about your bill. I'll pay whatever it costs to pull him through.'

Tom shook his head. 'That's not necessary, Marshal.'

'Well, that's decent of you. The way I see it, he's a witness to an attempted murder and the first thing we need to do is get him out of town, somewhere safe.' Rudd's heel squealed as he spun. 'Matt, can you take him with you to the L?'

Matt leaped forward. 'Sure. I'll fetch a wagon from the livery and—'

'Whoa.' Tom gripped Matt's shoulder, stopping him dead. 'He can't be moved. A simple bang on the head can do a lot of damage.' He glanced at Ros. 'It's anybody's guess what a bullet can do.'

Rudd pressed the heel of his hand to his forehead as he thought. It reminded Ros of somebody she'd known a long time ago, somebody she'd forgotten until recently. Jay Langerud. *No!* Emmett had put the seed in her mind and now it grew and flourished.

Rudd's voice dragged her back to the present. 'All right, you're the doc. Either way, I'll need to stay with him until he wakes up.' He was already shrugging out of his jacket and he tossed it on the foot of the bed.

'Make yourself at home. I can't offer you a bed, I'm afraid, but you're welcome to whatever else you need. I can bring some extra wood in for the stove.'

Unease twisted Ros's stomach in a knot and continued to tighten as she looked around. Tom nodded affably as he left to go on his new errand. Jake made no secret of checking the cylinders in his gun, then dimming the lamp before peeping between the curtains. Matt, she noticed, avoided eye contact, switching his attention neatly between Jake, Jimmy and the hallway. It was as though she were nothing more than a member of an audience watching a play she had no part in.

'Mind if I put in a few ideas?' she asked, quietly.

Rudd turned in her direction. 'I'd certainly expect you to.'

She took a deep breath, still rattled by the direction of her thoughts. Being home was like opening an old wound. If Rudd was indeed Jay Langerud, then he was the salt being rubbed into it.

'I don't think you staying with the boy is such a good idea. After what happened tonight, being around you might not be the safest place.'

She raised an eyebrow, challenging him to disagree. When he didn't, she continued with a little more confidence.

'Exactly what did happen tonight?'

Jake offered a shortened version of events that had transpired at the saloon before she arrived, while she endeavoured to keep her expression impassive. Listening intently was even more of a strain with her heart hammering hard enough to shake her teeth loose. Alternate waves of hot and cold washed over her. She was torn between pride and fear for Matt, disbelief and admiration for Rudd. When he finished, a pause

103

dragged the suspense out as she collected her mixed up feelings.

Eventually, she cleared her throat. 'And you said I was crazy. Looks as though we're two of a kind after all.' Unable to contain a smile, she peered towards Matt where he had withdrawn almost into the hallway and now stood furtively glancing along it. 'What do you have to say?'

She regretted the severity of her tone and across the bed she felt Rudd's gaze on her, warming her more than the stove was ever likely to. Lowering her eyes, she mumbled to soften her tone. 'Tell me where you stand in all this, Matt.'

He dropped his chin slightly but raised it quickly. This time his focus found Ros and stayed put. 'I told the marshal, and I'll tell you the same, this is a gun town. The only way to fight is to match fire with fire.' His fist tapped against his thigh, the only outward show of his frustration. 'God knows I've tried to follow Bill's example, turn the other cheek, but it hasn't made things better. Bill and May are still dead. Our cattle are still burning on the range. My men are still getting shot.'

Bitterness resounded in every tightly drawn word, pulling Ros's nerves taught as a bowstring. He was so young and yet he said 'my men' with the conviction of a man twice his age. It saddened her to see his youth stripped away, and yet, at the same time pride vied with fear and anger.

'So you and Rudd decided to start a war? Couldn't we at least have talked about it first?'

She thought about what Emmett had said, about giving Matt a fair chance. Would he take it? 'You don't have all the facts, Matt. There are things you need to know, things we need to talk about.'

Matt shrugged. 'I've done too much talking of late. This is my life, my town, my father's legacy. I want to live in a place where my wife and child can walk along the street and feel safe. Maybe it's not what you want, but somebody has to fight for it. Until tonight I didn't know how to do that.'

Ros scowled at Rudd. If he got her brother killed, she'd make sure he paid in kind. Apparently, Matt read her mind.

'Don't blame the marshal. He's the best thing to blow into this town in a while. He's what we need, somebody without a stake who can't be bought or threatened by Swain and his vigilantes.'

He hurt her with his contempt for her and his admiration for Rudd. She clenched her teeth and tried not to show it. Arguing would only drive a bigger wedge between them. Nothing she could say would undo the damage already done by years of sibling neglect, but that didn't mean she couldn't have the final word.

'All right, Matt, we'll play it your way. Just don't make the mistake of thinking I'm going to stand by and let you get killed.'

Matt lowered his gaze. 'I know that. I'm sorry, I—'

Ros interrupted his protests. 'Don't ever apologize to me. I've never had any time for sorry. If you have the conviction to do a thing, then at least have the dignity to live with the consequences.'

His mouth thinned to a tense line and this time his eyes narrowed when his glare locked on her. 'They were right, you are hard.'

They glowered at each other, but it was a struggle for Ros to maintain her outward show of cold composure. How could he be so wrong while at the same time forcing her to prove him right?

'Now, Matt, that's no way to speak to your long lost sister.'

The reprimand preceded the arrival of a pretty little blonde who slipped her arm through Matt's and smiled warmly at Ros. Surprise, curiosity and a sudden understanding brought Ros out of her chair as she sensed Rudd's amusement.

'You must be Ava.'

The blonde extended her hand as she met Ros halfway. 'I am, and I'm pleased to meet you. Are you all right after your ordeal? Did they hurt you?'

Ros clasped her fingers, wrong-footed by the girl's immediate friendliness and the swell of her stomach. She noted the wedding ring, quickly putting two-and-two together.

'I'm fine. They just wanted to talk. Why don't you sit down?'

'Actually, I am feeling a bit worn out. Have you finished with Matt?'

'We're finished,' Rudd said, quietly brooking no argument. 'It's been a long day. Doc, have you got a room they can have? I don't think it would be a good idea for us to split up tonight.'

'Sure.' He finished fastening his cuff. 'Come on, you

106

can have my mother's old room. Ros, you can have my room. I'll find a chair somewhere.'

Ros drew a steadying breath after they had all left, leaving her and Rudd alone. 'Don't think we're finished,' she warned him. 'I've still got something to say to you.'

A muscle twitched in his jaw as he stared at her, but she cut him off when he opened his mouth to speak.

'You get Matt killed, Rudd, and I'll—'

'I know what you'll do, you don't need to spell it out,' he said, calmly. 'I also know he's a good kid with enough responsibility and worry without you kicking his legs from under him every time you open your mouth. You should ease up on him.'

He was right but it didn't make the advice any easier to swallow. 'Do you think that's what Emmett's going to do? We're in a war. You included.'

He didn't deny it.

'So, as I was saying before, if you hide yourself in here, you'll be as good as telling Emmett you're not a man of your word. I very much doubt that's the case.'

He scowled. 'I'd like to argue that point . . . amongst others, but I can't. You're right.' He paced beside the bed, his attention on Jimmy who hadn't stirred despite the battle raging around him. 'I could get the sheriff to send over a deputy.'

'And frighten the kid to death when he wakes up?' Ros shook her head emphatically. 'We're all in this together now so I think I should sit with Jimmy for a while.'

'Offer accepted, but you look dead on your feet.' He

107

came round to meet her, extending his hand to draw her forward. 'I'll watch him for a few hours while you get some sleep. Maybe it'll improve your disposition.'

She glared at him as she stamped to the door, but turning to face him it was a struggle to keep her countenance sombre. 'Maybe this is my disposition. Did you think of that?'

His smile unnerved her, being all flashing teeth and mischief. He was a hard man to stay mad at.

'Then maybe Emmett Swain ain't the one we should be worrying about. Maybe you should think about that.'

Ros started to leave, but turned back. She should tell him what she knew, about him and her, and Radley and Parley Jones. The only problem was, she didn't understand it all herself and so far Rudd had been reluctant to tell her anything of substance. Right now, she was too tired to think about it.

CHAPTER 14

The following day passed slowly for Ros, marked only by the monotonous ticking of a long case clock in the hallway. A cold, crisp morning faded into a colder, darker afternoon as minutes slipped by like hours, each as long and boring as the last. To pass the time, Ros rested, disturbed by slight noises and the no-show of either Tom or Rudd to relieve her.

By early afternoon she paced like a caged lion in the narrow space between the bed and the stove, and cursed Rudd. She'd always hated time on her hands. It allowed doubts and worries to creep into her mind, raised questions that otherwise could have been conveniently overlooked.

She stopped mid-stride to watch Jimmy as he fretted in his sleep. Poor kid. His nightmares were as vivid as hers judging by his garbled ramblings. She only half listened as he raved about Emmett Swain and somebody called Cane or Cade. From the bits she had already pieced together, he'd seen and heard them plotting to run Rudd out of town. He also mentioned her brother Bill, shouting as though he were trying to warn him. Whether he was confused, or reliving the event, she could only guess, but her blood ran hot and cold with the torment.

'Ros. . . .'

Why would he be calling her name? She looked around the room, wondering whether Tom had managed to creep in and join them, but the room was as before, just the crackle and spit of the stove to keep them company.

'Matt. . . .' Jimmy mumbled.

She didn't want to hear her brother's name, not among a list of dead or marked men. Luckily, a knock at the bedroom door brought her attention and the pistol to bear on a suited man. He moved slowly to remove his derby hat, his gaze never leaving the gun, and inclined his head in greeting.

'Who are you? How did you get in?' Ros asked.

He pushed his small round glasses higher on his nose and started to move forward, stopping abruptly when he heard her cock the Colt.

'My name's Smith. Silas Smith,' he drawled. 'I work for Mr Burns the local attorney. He left some papers with me that he needs you to sign. Doc Bailey thought. . . .'

'I can't see you right now. I'm busy.'

He looked towards the bed. 'I'll try not to disturb the boy.'

'You'll have to come back. Whatever your business is I'm sure it can wait.'

'Not really. It concerns the Circle Double L.'

That piqued her curiosity and she looked him over.

He was about her height and build, with a weathered complexion and slicked back hair. The black leather case he clutched to his waist was stiff and polished. His hands were clean but his nails were dirty.

Something wasn't right.

'You should come back when the marshal's here,' she said, trying not to sound nervous.

'Oh no, Miss West, Doc Bailey said I could come on over when it suited and I'm afraid there's no time quite as convenient as now. You see, I have business out of town and if I don't get these papers signed before I leave . . .' He let the consequences hang. 'It won't take more than a few minutes. You're quite welcome to hold that gun on me for the whole time, if it makes you comfortable.'

He smiled, but it was too shallow to get to his eyes, more resembling a nervous flutter of his narrow lips, as though he wasn't quite as sure of himself as he wanted to sound.

'No. I think it would be better if you came back when the marshal is here.'

He moved as though he hadn't heard her, placing his case on the dresser near the window and rummaging inside until he pulled out a sheaf of papers. He gripped them close to his chest as he looked at her and cleared his throat.

'I only need a minute of your time and your signature on one paper.'

Ros looked nervously between the door, the window and the bed. Outside, a shadow passed the window, probably the deputy pacing. Sound asleep beneath a pile of blankets, Jimmy murmured and fidgeted.

Ros adjusted the weight of the Colt. Despite her bravado in front of Radley the day before, her fingers ached with stiffness.

'All right, let's get this over with, but keep your voice down. I don't want to wake the boy.'

She crossed the room to join Burns, relaxing the gun against her waist. Burns inclined his head in agreement as his gaze slid sideways to Jimmy.

'Let's get straight to business then.'

'Let's.'

He shuffled closer to Ros until their shoulders were almost touching.

'These are the pa—'

She inched away, offended by his sour odour.

'I can see you're in no mood for a lengthy explanation so I'll hurry things up.'

He shuffled the papers, drawing the top copies over to reveal a page at the back with a heavily dotted line. Reaching inside his bag, he withdrew an inkpot and pen, dipping the nib before he offered it to her.

'All you need to do is sign here and our business will be concluded.'

Ros hesitated.

'Is anything the matter?' He persisted with the pen, forcing it against her gun hand.

She snatched away, tightening her grip on the Colt. 'Aren't you supposed to tell me what I'm signing? I've changed my mind about you being here. You need to leave. I'm not signing anything. I want you to leave. Now.'

Dutifully, he packed the papers back into his bag, allowing his hand to linger inside. Behind her, Jimmy stirred and for a split second her attention faltered from Burns as she looked in the boy's direction. His eyes were staring while his mouth moved soundlessly and she went to him.

'It's all right, Jimmy. Stay still.'

He tried to move, but weakness and the tightly tucked bed held him. His breath hissed in shallow gasps as his eyes widened and glistened with fear.

'It's all right, Jimmy. Go back to sleep. '

Ros sat beside him, comforting him as best she could. She'd never spent much time around children or sick people and she felt the deficiency.

'See yourself out, Mr Smith,' she said, realizing her mistake as she heard the click of a hammer.

'I heard you were a stubborn bitch, but I really was hoping to make this as painless as possible for you. Thing is, you're not leaving me much choice. All you had to do was sign. Emmett Swain would have got your share of the ranch and—'

'C-Cade,' Jimmy stammered.

The Colt exploded in her hand. Glass shattered behind her. Smith – or Cade – fell back against the wall, blood spreading across his chest. His mouth opened in a question that wouldn't come. She cringed as his eyes stared past her for a moment, widening with surprise, then his lashes fluttered and he slumped to the floor.

CHAPTER 15

Over at Becky's café, Jake heard two shots close together, almost simultaneous. He rounded the bend in time to see Doc Bailey standing at the window, staring past the smashed glass. Running inside the house, he kept close to the walls, his gun preceding him before he ducked his head into each room. Nothing stirred and he gave a cursory check to the stairs as he passed *en route* to the sick room.

Finding a man slumped against the wall, Jake felt for a pulse in his neck. Amazingly, considering the blood covering his torso, he wasn't dead. Jake holstered his weapon then checked the wound. A .45 calibre judging by the size of the entry. Ros's shot had been true. It was a miracle he was still alive.

Jake stepped over the man's legs, ignoring him as his attention switched to Ros lying face down across Jimmy. The Colt lay several inches from her outstretched hand, and for a split second, he imagined the worst. A whimpering noise snapped him out of his initial shock and he shifted Ros carefully, relieved when he realized it was Jimmy he'd heard.

The boy stared past him with wide, liquid brown eyes, fear physically manifesting to rock his small body beneath the blankets.

'Easy, Jimmy. It's all right. You're safe.'

Doc Bailey joined them, immediately checking on the gunman.

'Try and keep him alive, Doc. I need him to help me put Swain away for good this time.'

'I'll do my best, but don't put money on it.'

Jake waved him away and knelt beside the bed. 'Is he the one, Jimmy? Was that the man who tried to kill me?'

The boy's mouth opened as though he might speak, but he couldn't seem to say a word. His breathing increased to short pants, his whimpers growing louder as his agitation mounted.

Jake's soothing did no good. The boy's anxiety heightened, his body jerking beneath the tightly tucked blankets as his eyes rolled and his gaze darted around the room – and then it was over. His eyes closed, his body went limp and he slipped into unconsciousness as suddenly as he had awakened. Jake leaned close, listening for his breath. It tickled his cheek and Jake relaxed a little, composing himself before he turned to Ros.

'You all right?'

She nodded, the fear in her eyes telling him more than she'd admit.

'Think you can help the doc?' he asked her. 'I need to sort out a few things here.'

She nodded and followed Tom as he hauled his

patient into the hallway.

'Marshal.'

Jake turned to face the deputy peering in through the window. The young man looked pale and confused as he rubbed the back of his head.

'What happened?' he asked.

'Where were you, Brady?' Broken glass crunched under Jake's boots as he stalked to meet him. 'I told you to watch the house. Why did you leave your post? Why did you let him in?'

'I've been out cold in the bushes. He tried to get in the house but I told him he couldn't go in. Then when I was walking round, checking to make sure everything was quiet, somebody hit me from behind.'

'And I suppose you didn't see who it was?'

Brady shook his head, winced and stopped. 'No, sir. The last person I remember seeing was him.'

Jake filed the information away for later. So far he had nothing to go on, except Swain's hatred of Ros. But the facts were too slow in coming, the motives vague. What he needed were hard facts and evidence, a lead that would help him make some sense of this crazy town and the people in it.

One thing at least was obvious: his control of the situation was dissolving quicker than snow in the sunshine. Also, the doc's house wasn't safe. He reached a snap decision and gave the deputy his full attention.

'Get this window boarded up.'

Deputy Brady gulped nervously, then spun on his heel and disappeared.

Jake glanced at Jimmy. The boy was sleeping, but his mouth moved constantly with whatever nightmare haunted him. Unfortunately, it was impossible to make out anything more than a whimper, which was more than could be said for the argument raging along the hall.

Jake moved to stand in the doorway, unwilling to leave Jimmy alone, but intrigued by the furore.

'You can't leave,' Tom shouted.

'I sure ain't staying here waiting to be murdered. Me getting shot at has become a daily occurrence.'

'What about Matt? You can't just run away again.' Tom's voice was thick with anger. 'He needs you, more now than ever with Bill gone.'

'Matt seems to be doing fine. He doesn't need me with a wife and a child on the way.'

'God, you sound bitter. Has it got that bad for you?'

'What do you mean?'

'Have you forgotten what it's like to be happy, if not for yourself, for somebody else?'

Something clattered. 'Happiness is for fools. Survival is all that matters.'

'Then you keep your fight away from Matt and Ava because if anything happens to her and that baby he won't survive. Surely you remember what it means to value someone else's life above your own?'

Jake half expected to hear a slap, but instead, there was silence.

'I remember some of where it got me,' Ros said after a short while. 'Working for Emmett in a stinkin' saloon, too afraid to show my face back home, cut off

117

from my life like a mad dog.' Ros's voice grew louder as anger loosened her tongue. 'God only knows what else I did. Maybe it was so bad that's why I can't remember. I know I've been no angel since.'

Jake wanted to tell her she had nothing to be ashamed of. Somehow, he didn't think she'd believe him.

Bailey's approach was less gentle. 'Oh, stop it. Didn't you tell Matt that if you have the conviction to do a thing, then have the dignity to live with the consequences? You made your choice when you ran off after Emmett. Seems to me what's happening now is just more of those consequences.' There was a noticeable pause. 'And what about the marshal? Where does he figure in all this?'

A hesitation. 'I don't know.' Ros sounded calmer, disheartened. 'He's part of those missing memories. One thing I do know, he's in as much danger as I am. Anyhow, we're not talking about him.'

'Damnit!' Bailey stamped into the hallway, stopping abruptly when he saw Jake. 'Cade's dead. There was nothing I could do.' He pinched the bridge of his nose and took a couple of deep breaths. 'I'm not sure there's anything anybody can do.'

CHAPTER 16

Ros was standing beside the window, itching for a fight when Jake joined her. 'Shut the door. I've got a message for Jay Langerud,' she said, glancing at him.

He met her straight on, not even an eyelash fluttering to betray what effect her revelation had on him. 'He's been dead a long time,' he said, coolly.

'That's not what Emmett told me.' She took a deep breath, but it did nothing to fortify her flagging spirits. 'Whether or not you want to admit who you are, you're in this deep.'

She hesitated. Her troubles were enough to bear without bringing his into the mix. But if he lived long enough, he might be the extra gun she needed in a fight. And there was a fight coming, sure as night followed day.

She considered her next words carefully. 'I didn't know if I could trust you before but it's not just about my survival now. There's a war coming, and whether you like it or not, you're on my side unless you saddle a fast horse and ride the hell away from here.'

His face darkened with curiosity. 'That's big talk and

war's a strong word. What did Swain say to you last night?'

'He wants the L, but I already knew that.' She hesitated, annoyed by his nonchalance, but sure about getting his full attention. 'He talked about what happened in Hays.'

Jake's brow arched in a question.

'He said when he tells Radley that the man who killed his pa, Parley Jones, is in town. . . .'

She left him wanting to know more. Wanting to know more herself as suspicion that he was Jay Langerud shaped into certainty.

'Radley is Parley Jones's son?' he asked.

The unspoken admission of his identity jolted her memory as surely as a bolt of lightning. She relived the nightmare of a corpse lying face down at the bottom of a ravine. Blood soaking the back of a pale blue shirt stretched tight across broad shoulders. She remembered running from the scene, back to a hotel, and packing her bags. She'd meant to leave, but there'd been a full bottle of whiskey on the dresser and she'd drunk it all until it numbed the pain and washed away the picture imprinted behind her eyelids.

Later, when she woke from a drunken stupor, she knew what she had to do. The clock struck twelve as she banged the door behind her and ran to the stage stop. She bought the last ticket, then fidgeted impatiently on the edge of the boardwalk as she waited for the coach. Someone told her the stage was always late, and she started to pace. A few feet. A few yards. Further. Willing the carriage to appear. The reverberation of hoofs and the creak of wheels announced its arrival as it thundered into town, six powerful horses foaming at the bit while the driver yelled for clear passage through. She started to run, back to her bags, jostled by a crowd of people gathering to meet the new arrivals.

Suddenly, someone shoved her in the back. She careered into the road. The driver hollered and hauled back on the reins but it had little effect on slowing the racing team. In her imagination, she could hear them snorting, see their nostrils flare—

'Ros!'

She shoved Rudd away as he tried to get hold of her. 'I'm all right.'

'Good. I thought I'd lost you there for a minute. Somewhere between you saying Radley was Jones's son and . . .' He stroked her cheek and she realized she was crying. 'Come on, sweetheart, it's all right. Don't cry about what's past. Jay died a long time ago, but me and you, we're still very much alive.'

She walked away from him, rubbing her hand across her eyes to hide the tears. 'You left me. Why? If I hadn't seen that body, Jay's body, I wouldn't have been anywhere near that coach.'

'It's a long stor—'

She threw him a warning glare. 'Stop it! If you're really in this with me, I want the truth. I want to know why I thought you were dead, why you never tried to find me.'

For a minute, the self-assured veneer peeled. 'I wasn't who you thought I was.'

'Well now I don't know who you are or who you were, so you might as well tell me everything.'

He stalked to the desk, aimlessly shifting papers and books. 'All right, but it won't make sense and you won't like it. I was a gunfighter working for Sheriff Riley. He asked me to join a gang that had been robbing stages and leaving bodies all over Kansas.'

His story came as an anti-climax and she couldn't keep the disdain from her voice. 'You couldn't have told me that? We were as close as two people can be and yet you couldn't trust me with the fact that you were a good man and not some . . . some murdering outlaw!'

She expected a heated argument, wanted one, but all she got was a weary sigh.

'You weren't truthful with me either.' He laughed sardonically and started pacing, for once looking more prey than predator. 'You never told me where you came from, about your family, why you were dealing blackjack in a saloon when every swing of the doors made you tremble in your satin shoes. For all I knew, you could have been part of the gang I was trying to smash.'

Realization made her chuckle. 'So that was the lie. I never meant a thing to you. I was just . . . a suspect.'

'No. That's not what I said. How could I tell you I was working with the law when you were obviously running from something you didn't want to confide in me?'

His logic infuriated her as much as the fact that she couldn't recall the details of anything he'd told her.

She wanted to shake him, force him into doing the same to her and rattle down the door that refused to let her through to the truth. Instead, she hurled her anguish at him.

'You're very smooth, Mr Rudd,' she said, chuckling ironically. 'It's easy to see how a frightened girl could fall in love with a man like you.'

He stopped walking and stared at her. 'You remember you loved me?'

She hesitated, giving his question more consideration than it needed. How could she say she'd loved a man she didn't recall as more than a dead body or a few shadows in her imagination?

'I'm guessing a frightened girl loved a dead gunfighter,' she said, hiding her feelings behind a matter-of-fact tone. 'Nothing more. Now if you'll excuse me, I need to find my brother and tell him we're leaving.'

She tried to get out before he stopped her, but he grabbed her arm. 'Hold on just a minute. You can't just swing in here and start giving him orders as though you own the—' He bit his lip. 'What I mean to say is, you've been gone a while and Matt's been running the ranch; can't you at least give him a chance to say his piece before you pull the rug out from under him again?'

She scoffed. 'Don't be so dramatic. He's just a kid, seventeen. And, don't forget, he's the one who brought me back here.'

'Now who's being dramatic?'

'All right, a simple question then: what do you think

he knows about fighting?'

His fingers bit into the tender flesh around her wrist, making her wince, but it didn't weaken his grip or his temper. 'What do you know? You've always run away from trouble. You were running the first time I met you and it looks to me as though you've been running ever since.'

She hesitated, thrown off balance by the derision in his accusation. 'You sound pretty sure about that. Maybe you're the reason.' She took a deep breath and stared at him. 'Why don't we get it all out in the open while we're being so honest? Go ahead. Tell me, what is it I've been running from?'

She saw temptation flicker in his eyes. He wanted to tell her the truth, and the red in his cheeks proved he was just about mad enough to do it. Instead, he took a deep breath and spoke gently. 'I remember you used to tread more carefully on people's feelings. Seems to me you were a stronger person for it.'

She ignored the insult. 'So you think I should back off, let Matt handle it alone?'

'That's not what I said. If you want my advice, you'll ease off, sit down and give Matt a chance to tell you what he wants to do, find out who he is, not who you think he is.'

'He's a fancy talker, isn't he?' Matt said, killing her argument as he filled the doorway. He swept off his hat and peeled off his gloves. 'Makes a lot of sense too. I think I should have some say in what's happening around here.'

She was cornered and she knew it. The fight left her

quick as a random thought, but she stayed focused, betraying nothing when she looked Matt in the eye.

'I agree with everything you've both said, but this is about more than the L. How much more I'm not sure, but taking one thing at a time, I guess I should really find out what you wanna do.' She faltered, her gaze flickering between Matt and Jake. 'Emmett made us an offer.'

'An offer?'

'We can let him have the L and you and Ava can ride out of here, or he'll take it.'

'Let him have your ranch?' Jake chipped in.

'Just like that,' Matt added incredulously. 'Who the hell does he think he is?'

Her composure crumbled a little more. Beneath Jake's fingers, still wound tightly around her wrist, her hand trembled.

'There's something you should know about Emmett.' She choked on the truth. 'He's our brother – half-brother.'

The denial was unanimous between Jake and Matt.

'Yes. That's why he left Langley, why our father gave him a thousand dollars to leave and start a new life.'

'No,' Matt said again.

'It's true. When Pa stopped me from marrying him, he said it was because he couldn't be sure. I believed he was wrong, that's why I left, followed Emmett halfway across the country. But when I caught up with him, he showed me a letter from Pa saying he was sorry for what he did and offering him a thousand dollars to stay out of our lives. I didn't want to believe it, but he had proof.'

Matt's feelings were as easy to read as an open book. Disbelief. Denial. Wonder.

Finally, he said, 'I don't blame you for going after him, but why didn't you come back when you found out the truth?'

She didn't know, and she couldn't help thinking her silence condemned her. Frustration settled in a hard knot in the pit of her stomach. Maybe she couldn't get those years back, but if she could recall them, maybe it would at least help to lay some ghosts to rest.

'I don't know.' She glanced towards Jake, looking for answers, but his expression was guarded.

Matt started to back away. 'Sorry. I just thought . . . well . . . it's none of my business. I guess I just wanted a reason not to believe. . . .'

'It's all right, kid. Maybe this is as good a time as any to get everything out in the open.' Jake's gaze held on Ros, his last words meant for her more than Matt, she was sure. 'I might be able to fill in some blanks. What is it you want to know?'

Matt stopped, his attention darting from one to the other, before settling on Jake. 'We heard stories after Ros left . . . lies about the life she was leading. They said she was shacked up with a gunfighter, working in a saloon and—' He jammed his hands into his pockets. 'I thought they were lies but after what I just over-heard. . . .'

Jake slowed his answer, suddenly bound to tell the truth, yet obviously nervous about riling Matt or Ros when their mood was already uncertain. 'It's not the way it sounded.'

Matt looked to the sky, a sigh punctuating the tension that worked the muscles in his jaw. He'd obviously been fishing for a denial. Ros on the other hand, hung on Jake's every word, her brows drawn into a tight frown.

'She dealt blackjack in the saloon, nothing more. I know that's the truth because I was the gunfighter she came back to every night.'

Matt's jaw dropped. 'You? But you're a United States marshal.'

'It's easy to make mistakes when you're young, kid. I was lucky, two good things happened to me: one was Sheriff Riley, the other was Ros.'

'Our Sheriff Riley?' Matt asked.

'That's right. He threw me in a cell one night when I was too drunk to hold my gun let alone draw it. Probably saved my life. When I sobered up, he told me he was gonna give me a chance to cut loose from the rut I was in if I wanted it bad enough.'

'He gave you a new name and a new start,' Ros finished with inevitability.

'No. He didn't make it that easy. He had a job that needed my particular talent with a gun, and my reputation. Doing that job was the first time I met Emmett Swain . . . and Ros.'

The knot in her stomach tightened some more bringing with it a swell of despair. 'Why can't I remember? I need to. I can't go on this way with every day bringing a new surprise!' Ros held up her hand for silence. 'No, stop there. There are probably things Matt doesn't need to hear.' She turned to her brother.

127

'Please, Matt, don't ask him anymore.'

Matt placed his gloves neatly together, giving it some thought. 'It seems there are things you two need to sort out. I shouldn't worry about the past, only be happy you're back. After all, I'm the one who refused to believe you were dead. Every morning since you left, I've stood on the L and waited for you to come home.'

Some of the uneasiness lifted.

'You always did follow me round like a homeless puppy.' She hadn't given a thought for anybody else when she upped and left, but at least now she had a second chance to make amends, if Emmett didn't kill her first. 'So, what are we gonna do?'

'Well, a third of the L probably belongs to Swain.' Matt stopped playing with his gloves. 'Did Bill know?'

Ros shrugged. 'Not when I left'

'If Pa had told us, things might be different. Bill and May might still be here. You never would have run away.'

'You don't know that. I thought I loved Emmett.' She glanced uneasily at Rudd and saw him frown. 'I would have followed him anywhere, done anything for him.'

'What about now? Do you want to give him his share?' Matt asked.

There was only one reason why they should – blood. But she could think of a few reasons not to, or at least doubts that begged an explanation. For starters, what had he done to make her hate him? And what had she done that he wanted her dead?

'I might have, before he murdered Bill and May,

before he tried to have me killed and stole my memories, but not anymore.'

'What do you mean he tried to have you killed?' Jake asked.

'The other night at the Crystal Slipper, Emmett admitted he was the one who pushed me under that stagecoach.'

Matt's eyes narrowed, his gaze taking on a faraway quality as he scowled. He reminded Ros of their father, a mild-mannered man until the gates of fury opened. Had Matt also inherited his murderous temper?

She took a deep breath. 'It's up to you, Matt. You've got more of a stake in the L than I have. I'll fight 'til my last breath to keep it, if that's what you want, but if it's not, tell me now. I've already wasted too much of my life on lost causes.'

He considered for a minute, his gaze turning towards the hall where the sound of a door opening heralded the arrival of a visitor. 'One way or another, Swain's tried to destroy this family and I think it's time to settle the score, I really do.' He wrapped his arm around Ava's expanded waist as she joined him. 'But truthfully, I'm scared. I don't want to risk losing Ava or the baby.'

Spontaneously, Ava wrapped her arms around him and squeezed tight. Ros envied them at that moment. They all might die when the fighting started, and that fear made her yearn for the intimacy Matt had with his pretty wife.

She twisted free of Rudd. 'You and Ava stay here, lock the doors, keep away from the windows. You'll be safe. We're going out for a while.'

'Where?' Rudd asked, following her as she shoved past her brother.

'Somewhere I can find answers.'

CHAPTER 17

The clerk at the hotel looked surprised to see them then scowled when Ros asked for Rudd's room key. Someone had repaired the door, re-hung it at least, but the splintered wood was still a stark reminder of the previous shenanigans. Ros swung it open and marched into the familiar room. Rudd followed close on her heels, the door slamming behind him, a testament to his mood though he hadn't said a word on the way over.

For a while, they stood on opposite sides of the room, staring at each other.

'Any reason you came back here?' Jake asked.

'Tom said something intense might trigger my memory. This seemed as good a place as any. It seems you and me have quite a history in hotel rooms.'

She sighed, the chill in the air cooling her enthusiasm for an idea that suddenly lacked good judgement. After all, she'd lived years without caring what was missing from her memory. Did she really need to know now? Nothing he'd said to Matt had even tickled her memory. Wasn't it enough to know she was in danger?

131

A knot of anxiety twisted in her stomach. 'It seems I'm not the whore I thought. I'm sorry. Was I always this stupid?'

He laughed, easing the tension as he invited her to sit with him on the bed. For the first time since she'd met him again, it felt comfortable.

'You know, I don't think Emmett's as interested in the ranch as he was. When we showed up it stopped being about just taking what he thought he had a right to. That night, when he had me at the Slipper, he talked about me betraying him . . . and how you and I had cost him three years of his life. Do you know what he meant?'

He sat beside her, his mouth pressed into an unyielding line. Minutes passed and still he said nothing.

'All right,' she said, 'I'll start. I've had a nightmare since I woke up after my accident. I see a man's body at the bottom of a ravine. I run away, back to a hotel and pack my bags. I run to the stage stop. I buy the last ticket. Someone tells me the stage is always late and I start to pace. Willing it to arrive. Then it does. I start to run, jostled by the crowd. Suddenly, I'm shoved in the back and. . . .'

Her voice had grown to a crescendo and she forced it back to calm. 'You know the rest. It's your turn now. Tell me who I've been mourning and why and what it has to do with Emmett.'

Jake picked up her hand and clasped it against his thigh. 'Ros, I'm sorry. If I hadn't let you leave that day. . . .'

His reasons remained unspoken, a secret as they sat quiet, both looking at their intertwined hands. In the end, Rudd broke the silence.

'The gang I was running with was led by a man named Jim West.'

'West?' She balked at the coincidence.

'That last night, you'd been dealing blackjack in the Golden Nugget and I was playing stud at a table in the back. I saw West come in, but it wasn't me he was looking for. He checked, but he didn't see me behind the beaded curtain, then when I saw him take you aside I got curious. I thought he was going to hurt you so I followed. He took you to a storeroom, but before I busted in I heard you laughing. There was a window, so I climbed up and. . . .'

'And what?' she asked, impatiently.

The confidence she'd grown accustomed to seemed to leave him and his voice lacked its usual warmth when he found the words to continue.

'He told you to forget about me, said he'd give you a ticket out of there. I didn't understand, thought he was threatening you until you hugged him, saying how happy you were.' He shook his head in bitter denial. 'You and me were close as ticks on a dog's back, but it seemed you and West were closer. I don't mind telling you I was mad, and jealous as hell. I ran out of there and went back to the hotel, only by the time I got to our room I'd convinced myself he was playing you. I was sure he must be threatening you, using something against you to get to me. After all, you were my girl, who better to find out what I was doing and let West know.'

She felt the weight of her betrayal on him. He'd warned her about opening up old wounds, trying to discover the past too quickly. Selfishly, she'd assumed he was worried about her feelings, but the facts shifted the burden of guilt.

'I'm sorry, Jake.' She wondered why she was apologizing for something she didn't remember, but his sullen look seemed to mirror her own disbelief.

'There was nothing you could have told him. You didn't know about me and Sheriff Riley because I never told you anything. I thought it would be safer that way.'

Her relief was short-lived, denial bringing her to her feet. 'But I must have known. Why else would West have seduced me?'

'Believe me, you couldn't have known. The only other person who knew was Riley and he was in Texas.' He shook his head, dismissing any further argument. 'Anyhow, by the time you got back that night, I'd decided what I was going to do. The next day we were gonna get out o' town. To hell with Riley. I'd start a new life somewhere else, where nobody knew Jay Langerud and a man and his wife could make a good life.'

'So you asked me to marry you.'

Somehow the idea appealed to her and she pictured Matt and Ava. Could she have been as happy as they were?

'No. I never got around to it. You were hysterical when you came in. You said you had something to tell me, wouldn't quieten down until you did. Turned out

134

you'd heard West arranging a surprise for me out at Danson's Rock. That's why he wanted you out of town, so you couldn't spoil it.'

'If you knew it was a trap, why did you go?'

He glanced up, predatory yellow eyes fixing her with suspicion. 'How do you know I was talking about a trap?'

'Your tone suggested it.'

'Mm. Well, you're right.'

She let out her breath. With the tension mounting, she was starting to mistrust herself, confusing guess-work for knowledge. Maybe she'd lost her memory along the way but she'd never lost her feeling of moral-ity. And from the first time he accosted her in this hotel room she'd felt a sense of belonging when she was with Jake.

'Only instead of running,' he said, 'I decided to walk right into it. West was robbing stages and leaving bodies all over the territory. I wanted to send him to prison where he couldn't hurt or kill any more inno-cent people.'

She was only half listening as she wondered how she could have got mixed up with a murderer. And where had Emmett been while all this was going on?

'What is it?' Jake asked.

'What you said about me and West . . . it bothers me. If you and I were lovers, I don't believe I would have betrayed you with another man. I know I'm not that kind of woman.'

'We all do things we regret from time to time,' he said philosophically.

'Agreed, but I spent nearly three years in a whore-house. I know my limits.' She read confusion in his expression. 'The Mission of St Mary? You assumed it was a religious sanctuary and I wasn't in the mood to correct you.' Standing up, she began to pace. 'But now things have changed. I've got questions of my own, starting with who West was and what he might have had over me.'

Jake's breath formed a cloud as he exhaled loudly. 'This is where things get complicated.'

She stopped and looked askance, a hint of amuse-ment easing some of her tension. 'You mean they're not already?'

He didn't indulge her attempt at humour. 'I've seen West recently.'

Before she asked, she had a feeling she knew what he'd say. Emmett had as good as admitted he pushed her under that stagecoach. The only flaw in his confes-sion had been his reasons for doing it. Jake saved her the trouble of wasting a question.

'You'd know him better as Emmett Swain.'

The knowledge winded her. 'That explains a few things. Why else would Emmett push me under that stage?'

'Bastard.' Jake reached up and pushed the hair away from her face, tracing the white scars etched into her forehead. 'If for nothing else, I'll kill him for that.'

Ros met his glare with a shiver of trepidation. He'd shown compassion to a boy, friendship to her brother and stayed with her when she needed him. But when the layers of affability were stripped away, the killer beneath shone bright as polished steel.

Still, everything considered, he didn't frighten her. Whatever happened, he wouldn't use his anger against her. Suddenly, the feelings she'd tried to deny smothered her. She slipped her hands around his neck, tentatively feathering kisses on his mouth until they softened the anger that had turned him to steel.

'There's no going back now,' he mumbled, as he kissed her.

'I know. Emmett said we were living on borrowed time.'

'What else did he say?'

She stopped and thought for a minute. 'He said you had a lot of forgiveness in you.'

She swung round and sat on the edge of the bed next to him. For a long time she couldn't say anything as an inexplicable feeling of foreboding crept over her.

'Will you do something for me?' she asked.

His eyes narrowed.

'Take your jacket off and turn around.'

It was a simple enough request, yet she sensed reluctance. 'Please, there's something I need to know.'

He turned his back towards her and faced the window. His reflection in the dark glass showed fear. Without being asked, he lifted his shirt. Winter had brought the night in early and she moved in close, smoothing her hand across his back . . . and a scar the size of bullet wound.

'I did that?'

He let his shirt drop and faced her. 'You thought you were shooting Parley Jones.'

'Parley Jones . . . but Emmett said you. . . .'

'Remember the trap West was laying for me? Well, I got the jump on Jones that day, switched my clothes and hat with his and marched him out into the ambush. West was up in the rocks somewhere and he shot the man he thought was me.'

'So Emmett shot you. He was lying when he blamed me.'

Jake frowned. 'I could let you believe that, but later when you've had time to think about it, the doubt'll drive you mad. He shot Jones thinking he was me. When I turned to get a shot off at him, you fired.'

She jumped to her feet, refusing to believe it. 'But I saw your body in the ravine. I know I did. It's all I've dreamed about.'

He grabbed her arm, stepping in close as she tried to run from him. 'It was Jones. Same hair, same build, same clothes. Believe me, I wish I had no memory of it, especially at night when I wake up in a cold sweat, shaking until the whiskey kicks in, wishing it had been me.'

'Why?'

'Because I've never forgotten that look on your face when you turned around and saw me on the ground and realized what you'd done. You thought I was dead and I was too weak to tell you otherwise. That's why you ran.'

She wrapped her arms around him, her fingers tracing the outline of the scar she'd caused. In her lowest times she'd never imagined anyone else might be living a nightmare equally as terrifying as hers, or that the truth might be worse than the dream.

'I'm sorry, Jake,' she said over again.

He kissed her as though he might take the pain away, hard and soft, long and slow. Beneath her hands, his muscles strained as his mouth sought the taste of her and together they peeled away the last barriers between them.

She let the final layers drop away, relishing her newfound liberation. For a long time she'd been crippled by guilt and ashamed of her disfigurement. The horses' hoofs had left their imprint on her body and her mind, leaving scars to hide behind like a shield. As Jake's eyes and hands and lips found each imperfection, she revelled in the beauty and freedom he gave her. For a short while, there was no past and no future, only a shared moment in time.

CHAPTER 18

The sky hung grey and foreboding and ice formed a new frame around the window. It took a minute or two before Jake rolled out of the warm blankets, tearing himself away from the softness of the woman beside him. Landing silently on his knees beside the bed, he tugged on his socks then tiptoed to the dresser to throw water over his face. Glimpsing himself in the crazed mirror hung on a nail buckled into the wall, he stroked his beard thoughtfully. It felt thick and unkempt and, searching under the bed, he found his carpetbag and inside a change of clothes and his shaving gear.

After stropping the blade, he lathered his face with soap and drew the razor precisely across his cheek. As the beard disappeared, he heard movement behind him and glanced around, wary of the response he might get. She hadn't remembered anything last night despite everything he'd told her and the familiarity between them that had come as easily as breathing. Still, awakening dormant memories might be more than she could handle coming on top of everything else. However, for now, Ros stayed asleep curled into a ball beneath the blankets, which wound tightly around her.

Jake chuckled as he stroked off the last of his beard and splashed his face. He'd forgotten she snored. Forgotten a lot of things. Like the way she enjoyed sleeping with her back curled against his front. How good she made him feel, as though he'd do anything for her.

He ran his fingers across his bare cheek. It felt strange after hiding behind whiskers for so long, but a lot had changed in the hours between dusk and dawn. Now all that remained was to finish his transformation. Quickly, he changed into something more practical than the suit he favoured; rough cotton trousers, a blue calico work shirt and a black leather vest. As he finished dressing, Ros rolled onto her back and opened her eyes, lids fluttering.

'Good morning.'

Jake finished fastening his pants as he bent over and kissed her on the lips. 'Good morning, sweetheart.'

Sighing deeply, she rubbed the last of the sleep from her eyes. 'I hardly recognize you without the whiskers.'

He rubbed a palm across his naked cheek and grinned, deepening the dimples at the corners of his mouth. 'Does it stir any memories?'

She pulled him down to sit beside her, her fingers tracing the outline of his jaw as her gaze scrutinized every feature of his face. 'Still nothing. Sorry.' She stretched, then curled up under the blankets. 'It doesn't matter though. Last night was the first time, the last time and every time in between. I know what I feel.'

'Is that so?'

'Yes. I also know what I want do about the L, Matt and Emmett.'

Her announcement caught him off guard and he couldn't help thinking she'd make an excellent lawman the way she switched seamlessly from one issue to another.

'I'm listening,' he said.

'After what you told me, I know this trouble with Emmett is not about the L any longer. Agreed?'

He nodded, wondering what was coming.

'Whatever happens, Emmett wants us dead. Right?'

'That's a given. Are you going somewhere with this?'

She dallied a while longer. 'I came back here because Matt placed an advertisement, calling me back, and I didn't know what else to do. I didn't want to be here, didn't have a stake. My father told me never to come back. If I hadn't been afraid for myself, hadn't felt something good in you, I would have left that first night.' She clasped his hand. 'That's not why I'm staying anymore. You've brought out a side in me I'd chosen to forget. Don't make me spell it out.' The wretched look in her eyes implored him. 'I want Matt and Ava and their unborn child to have a long life together. I don't want him to die because of something I did . . . or we did, you and me. Do you understand?'

The feeling of anticipation that had come over him the night he confronted Swain in the Crystal Slipper, engulfed him again. Only now, he was starting to like the prospect of trouble. It blew away the cobwebs that had gathered on his comfortable life, made the blood pump faster through his veins. More than that, it identified his purpose, his reason for being who he was – gunfighter, lawman.

'I think so,' he said. 'But before we leave this room, I think there's something we need to get straight.'

'What?' she asked, a slight stammer betraying the real depth of her anxiety.

He kissed her, lingering as he spoke. 'I want you and me to have a life together when this is over, maybe even have what Matt and Ava have.'

Her eyes widened, telling him more than anything she might say. Despite their differences, her missing memory and the direness of their current situation, the feelings and dreams they'd shared before were still alive.

'You mean family?'

He fought to keep his composure as the word exploded a deep-rooted yearning in his belly. 'If we're going to do this crazy thing, it's got to be worth fighting for. Agreed?'

She curled her fingers in his hair, holding him close. 'Agreed. Thank you, Jake. Thank you for everything. Let's go and tell Matt, get this over with. I need to start the rest of my life as soon as I can.'

'Tom? Matt?' Ros called as they entered the doc's house.

Nothing seemed out of place but a feeling that something wasn't right made Ros and Jake draw their guns at the same time. They looked at each other, then

143

spread out along the hallway, Jake checking the rooms to the right while Ros peered into the kitchen and up the stairs.

She gasped when she turned and glimpsed Tom unconscious on the floor. Jake ran past him and, as she followed him into Jimmy's room, Ros saw Ava bound to the head of the bed by her wrists. Jimmy clung to her skirt, his cheek buried against her leg where she knelt beside him. Behind a thick rag tied around her mouth, Ava's pale skin glistened and her red eyes flooded with tears. When Jake untied her, she collapsed against him, releasing a tirade of sobs she seemed unable to stop despite the gasps of air she sucked in.

Ros knelt and examined the back of Tom's head where blood matted his hair. He groaned, shoving her hand away as she turned him over and helped him to sit. His eyes were cloudy, confusion and pain adding to the certainty that he'd received a heavy blow.

'What happened? Where's Matt?' she asked, as he reeled between her and the wall.

'Radley and Carson took him. There was nothing we could do. They rushed in from the back, had us dead to rights before we knew what was happening. I couldn't take any chances with Ava and the baby and the boy.'

'Where have they taken him? Why?' She almost shook him.

'They were looking for you and the marshal. We didn't know where you were.'

Ros glanced guiltily at Jake as he left Ava nursing a glass of water and came to lend a hand with Tom. He squeezed her shoulder briefly, then hauled the doc to his feet and circled his waist supportively before sitting him on the end of the bed.

'Did they say anything else?' he asked calmly.

Tom nodded and groaned as the pain hit him. Ava pushed in between them. She sniffled as she examined his wound.

'They want you two,' she murmured. 'Said they couldn't be sure that you wouldn't just leave town. Took Matt as an in . . . in . . . cen . . .' She fought hard not to start crying again but the words couldn't break through. 'Would you? Would you just leave us . . . would you?'

The utter devastation in Ava's voice broke through Ros's anger. 'No. We'd never do that. We've been . . .' Ros drew breath on the details. 'We came to tell you and Matt that we were going to take care of everything – Emmett – that you didn't need to worry. We've got a plan. I didn't want you and Matt getting caught up in all this. Please, Ava, believe me, I didn't.'

Ava nodded, her whole body rocking with the movement. 'But surely you're the one being caught up. If Matt hadn't placed that advertisement. . . .'

Ros's liking for the girl deepened. Even with Matt in danger she was defending Ros.

'Don't feel any sympathy for me, Ava. I don't know what Matt told you, but me and Emmett go back a long way. What's happening now, it isn't about ownership of the L. You said they came for me and the marshal . . .' She glanced in his direction. 'Jake,' she corrected. 'The truth is, we've been in this situation with Emmett before. Only difference this time is Matt got caught up in something he shouldn't.'

Tom wrapped his arm around Ava as a fresh flood of tears gushed down her cheeks. 'I didn't know you had it in you, Ros,' he said. 'The marshal's obviously good for you. You said you've got a plan. Whatever it is, I'm in.'

'Me, too. You fools want to tell me what the hell's been happening around here?' The sheriff leaned breathlessly against the wall. Over his usual mismatch of clothes and patches he wore a sheepskin coat with the collar pulled up. It didn't hide the torn shirt beneath or the blood oozing from a nick under his earlobe. 'I just got my ass kicked out of the Crystal Slipper. Saw Matt while I was there.'

'Is he all right?' Ava and Ros asked in unison.

'Tied to a chair, a few cuts and bruises that I could see. Swain sent a message for you two.' He looked between Jake and Ros. 'Says you've got twenty minutes to show your faces otherwise he'll start using Matt for target practice.'

The room stilled to an eerie quiet.

'You got plenty of ammo, Ros,' Jake asked without looking up from checking the tie on his holster.

She nodded solemnly as she loaded her gun from bullets in her coat pocket. 'More than enough now.'

CHAPTER 19

'Aren't you going to ask me if we're doing the right thing?' Jake asked, as he and Ros strode along Main Street, their pace slow but steady as they came in sight of the Crystal Slipper.

She kept her focus on the road ahead and the loafer leaning too casually against the hitch rail outside the saloon. He hardly seemed to notice their approach, but she had no doubt he knew exactly where they were, stride for stride.

'Are we?' she asked, her eyes narrowing as the idler flicked his unsmoked cigarette into the street.

'If we can get Radley and Swain out in the open, leave Clay Carson for Riley to pick off – assuming he and the doc make it through the back door – and hope that bartender doesn't have the balls to use that rifle he keeps under the bar . . .' He took a breath. 'Hell, yes.'

Ros couldn't help smiling at the inevitability in his answer. In reality the plan was flimsy at best. The back entrance to the saloon would probably be guarded. Matt could get caught in the cross-fire. Radley might be faster than Jake. Then again, even if Radley did get Jake, she'd put a bullet through him before she went down.

The loafer straightened up and stretched, glancing in their direction, then not so casually shouted, 'They're here, boss.'

Every muscle in Ros's body tensed. She wanted to look at Jake, walking shoulder-to-shoulder with her towards an uncertain outcome. But why? What if she read the same uncertainty in his expression that she felt in her belly?

'Are you sure you can handle Emmett?' Jake asked, slowing his pace and lowering his voice to no more than a whisper. 'It's not easy shooting a man.'

Ros's chest tightened when Radley wandered out and stood by the hitch rail. Emmett followed, standing apart from his paid gunman; out of any direct line of fire. Freshly barbered, wearing a dark suit and with his injured arm visibly supported in a decadent silk sling, his smile only added to Ros's disdain.

She sneered. 'He pushed me under a stagecoach, put a bullet in my back, then left me to die out in the middle of nowhere, or paid the man who did.' She sucked in a ragged breath. 'If it's you or him, I've got you covered this time.'

Jake chuckled, low down in his throat. 'You're gonna be a hell of a good wife.'

The sentiment warmed her. A woman could probably do just about anything for the love of a good man. She didn't have time to react with anything more than a feeling of lightness that swooped up from her feet and sailed through her to land in a twitchy smile on her stiff lips.

'I see you got my message,' Emmett shouted as they stopped within twenty feet. 'I wasn't sure you'd come.'

'Is Matt all right?' Ros asked.

Emmett pointed towards the saloon. 'See for yourself.'

The creaky old doors swung open as if on cue, enough to see some of what lay beyond. Matt slumped over, gagged and bound to a chair in the centre of the room – directly in the line of any fire. For one heart-stopping moment, Ros thought he was already dead, until Carson dragged him up by his hair and he groaned.

'Got anything to say to your sister?' the redhead asked, counting a second off before he punched Matt in the face, spraying blood across the floor as he laughed.

The doors swung shut, banging until their momentum died.

'I hate you, Emmett,' Ros said.

'Not yet you don't.' He glanced sideways at Radley, his grin widening as he took a step closer. 'But you will.'

'Don't let him rile you,' Jake said for her ears only. 'Keep a cool head, he won't be expecting that.'

The sound of Jake's voice, calm and collected, infused her with a measure of confidence. She gritted her teeth and nodded almost imperceptibly.

'I see you're still wearing your badge, Marshal,' Emmett shouted. 'I thought somehow it might have

149

disappeared along with your whiskers. By the way, it's nice to see you again, Jay.'

'I'm an optimist. I'm hoping we can settle this the right way.'

'Right for who? You?' Emmett snorted. 'Are you going to arrest yourself for murder?'

Ros's gaze flickered to the gunman who was methodically rolling a cigarette. He stared insolently at Jake, the mention of murder hardly registering behind the coolness of his ice-blue eyes. Emmett laughed, the overtly loud sound taunting as he leaned closer to Radley and whispered something. The blond's face stiffened, his fingers crushing the cigarette before it reached his lips. He started forward, but Emmett held him back.

'So, are you lawman or gunman today?' Emmett asked Jake.

'Will it make any difference?'

Radley's eyes narrowed. 'Not to me, you son-of-a-bitch.'

Jake unpinned his badge and tossed it. 'Stay away from me, Ros. I don't want you taking a stray bullet.'

Ros's knees wobbled as the strength seemed to drain out of her. She almost reached for the support of Jake's arm, but he sidestepped neatly away. When her eyes found his face, the cold killer she'd only glimpsed before had found his way to the surface. No more was he mild-mannered Jake Rudd, US Marshal. With his legs braced apart, back straight, eyes focused on the man moving out to meet him, he was one-hundred per cent Jay Langerud, gunfighter. She hardly recognized the drone of his voice.

'So, Radley, I'm guessing he just told you how I gunned down your pa. Told you how I shot him in the back and left him for the vultures? About now, you're probably thinking I'm not that fast.'

Radley stood straight, relaxed, his hand poised for the drop and sweep that would bring his gun up in a lightning quick movement. 'Maybe, if that's how it happened.'

Ros had been wondering when Riley would make his move, cause the diversion that would give Jake and her time. Now her attention strayed to Radley. He'd said 'if': was that doubt or a slip of the tongue?

Her gaze switched to Jake. He didn't move, didn't blink as he held Radley's piercing stare. If it hadn't been for the whiteness of his breath against the cold, she might not have believed he was alive.

'That's one version. Seems to me that's the one you'll want to believe.'

'To be truthful, you don't strike me as a man who'd shoot a rival in the back. On the other hand, I always wondered two things about Parley Jones. If he was really my pa, and whether he was good with a gun, or just lucky.'

'He sure wasn't lucky. The same ma—'

'Cut the talk, Radley,' Emmett shouted. 'It's time to do what I pay you for. Kill him.'

'Hold your horses, Mr Swain, it'll happen. I'm interested to know what the man has to say. Go ahead.'

'I said, your pa wasn't lucky. The same man who paid him, put a bullet in his back. You might want to remember that.'

Ros held her breath, tried to match Jake's cool demeanour but despite the cold, heat flooded her body leaving her flushed and dizzy. It was as though she was standing too close to a fire, mesmerized by the flames but driven back by the heat. And then, all hell broke loose.

It was too fast to say what happened first. Later, Riley would swear he and Tom stole in through the back door after the doc did some kind of stranglehold on the guard. Carson pulled his gun and Riley shot him. Matt threw himself down, taking the chair with him, upending a table and scattering the bystanders who'd come along for the show. The bartender thought about pulling his rifle but Riley's bullet shattering the mirror behind his head dispelled any real thought of heroics. A couple of others, easy money no-accounts, had surrendered on the spot. Doc Bailey had laid them out with a couple of punches then untied Matt.

All Ros knew for sure was Riley's first shot had been the surprise it was intended to be. Jake's Colt cleared leather at the same time as Radley's. The shots were close enough to sound like one. Ros didn't have time to worry. Her gun appeared in her hand before she had to time to think about drawing it, just about the same time something hard and sharp hit her in the side of the knee.

Her leg buckled, throwing her off balance as she squeezed off a shot at Emmett. She fell hard and rolled clumsily, saw Emmett flounder as she dropped her gun. Out of the corner of her eye, she glimpsed Jake fold at the middle, clutching his waist with both hands. A chill swept through her, her attention snapping to Radley as she scrabbled for her Colt.

He stood, rock-still, the iciness behind his eyes melting as he gloated at his handiwork. 'I guess I'm the lucky one today.'

A movement near his shoulder caught Ros's attention, fear freezing her limbs as Emmett staggered forward. The gun in his hand flared, but as he fired right at her, Radley careered between them. Emmett's shot hit him in the back, finishing the job Jake's bullet had started and affording her precious seconds as she clawed dirt and grabbed her Colt.

'You're dead,' Emmett shouted.

His features twisted in an ugly grin as he struggled to cock his weapon. Maybelle's bullet slowed him down, but not enough. He brought the muzzle up, levelling it on her as she brought up the Colt. A shot exploded, Ros staggered backwards, only it wasn't her who fell.

Emmett clutched his back, his eyes staring past her, the grin sliding from his face as his eyes widened with shock. He swivelled on his heel, swaying before he finally crashed to the dirt. Matt watched him fall, then stumbled against the hitch rail, Tom's shotgun falling from his grasp as he hung his head in his hands.

Ros started forward but an arm circled her waist, dragging her back against a hard body. She turned on a dime, stopping a split second before she would have emptied her pistol into the man holding her in a vice-like grip. Relief overwhelmed her.

'Jake? I thought. . . .'

He held up his hand, dripping blood. 'He was fast, like his pa. I guess bad luck just ran in the family.'

CHAPTER 20

The desk clerk at the hotel seemed pleased to see Ros and Jake when they strolled arm-in-arm into his lobby late that evening. Before Jake could ask for the key to their room, the gaunt faced man rushed round to meet them, his hand extended in a warm welcome.

'Welcome back, Marshal. It's good to see you again.' He glanced at Ros and smiled broadly. 'You too, Miss West.'

Jake held up his bandaged hand, excusing himself from a hearty handshake. 'It's sheriff now. Can we have our key?'

'Er . . . I . . . erm . . .' The clerk burst into nervous laughter. 'Of course, what am I thinking. Er . . . actually, I moved you to a nicer room. Also, I heard you were on your way over so I had some food sent up and a bath.'

'That's kind of you,' Ros said, warily.

'It's the least any of us can do after what you two did.'

'What we did?' Ros asked, still uneasy with the scene that had left Emmett, Radley and Carlson dead, Jake

155

nursing a busted hand and her brother bruised and battered.

'You gave us our town back.' He handed them a key on a brass ring, then backed away. 'Enjoy your evening, and if there's anything you need, just let me know.'

Around the lobby, doors that had creaked open now swung wide and faces appeared, young and old, men and women. Ros and Jake started up the stairs, baffled by the attention, especially when a ripple of applause followed them. When they reached the first and second floors, the reception was the same. By the time they reached their room, Ros was struggling to control a fit of laughter.

Jake opened the door, releasing the aroma of steak and gravy as it rushed to meet them like another round of applause. Pushing her way inside, Ros stood in the middle of the room, turning on her heel as she surveyed her grand surroundings. By the window, a small table laden with covered trays had been set with two places and finished with a bottle of wine and two glasses. A full tub stood at the foot of the bed, the faint scent of lavender competing with the smell of the food.

'Can you believe this?' Ros asked, throwing herself across the high bed covered with an elaborately detailed quilt. 'It's as though we did something . . . heroic.'

Jake seemed less impressed, his answer barely more than a casual observation. 'Swain hurt a lot of people. Some lost their livelihood to him, others lost their dignity, some even lost loved ones.'

Ros stopped laughing, the simple truth acting like a

slap in the face. 'I know how that feels. I'd love to have seen my brother Bill again, and my pa.'

Jake slowly untied and unbuckled his gun, laying it on the table next to the bed. 'Uh-huh.'

Ros lay on her side and propped herself up on one elbow, watching as he struggled to kick off his boots. He'd been subdued since the smoke cleared. They'd barely got a word out of him when they went back to Tom's house. The only spark he'd shown had been when Jimmy asked for him, the first coherent word the boy had spoken since Cade had tried to kill Ros. However, spending time alone with the boy seemed to have plunged Jake into a deeper silence.

Now, kicking off his boots, he stretched out on the bed and closed his eyes, effectively shutting her out. He started to wedge his hands behind his head but reconsidered and rested his injured right hand across his chest.

Ros adjusted her position, rolling onto her stomach, leaning on her elbows, hands forming a rest under her chin as she watched him. Below a frown, dark shadows ringed his eyes and stubble darkened his jaw. It seemed to underline the mood that had come over him since the showdown with Radley.

'Jake.'

He didn't move.

'Are you all right?'

He took a breath but didn't say anything.

'Want something to eat?'

He shook his head, his mouth tightening into a line.

'Want to tell me what's wrong?'

Silence.

'Please, Jake. Is it something I've done? Something I've said?' Cold dread made her work harder. 'Have you changed your mind about us?'

He opened his eyes and smiled at her. It was a strange smile that seemed to dip the corners of his mouth instead of raising them. A sad smile. 'No. I'm just tired, that's all.'

She lay down, resting her cheek on his chest, listening to the steady rhythm of his heart. Beneath her palm his muscles felt tense as she caressed his stomach. Even his breathing sounded loud in the quiet of the large room. Suddenly, his hand came around her shoulders, hugging her tighter, as though he were worried she might leave if he didn't hold her.

'Jake, I think there is something bothering you. Can't you tell me what it is?'

He pushed up into a sitting position, his back rigid against the wrought-iron bedstead. 'What I did today bothers me.'

Ros waited, but that appeared to be all he had to say. 'You rid the town of a killer.'

'Did I?'

'Of course you did. Radley's dead. Emmett's dead. Carlson, if you want to include him. Who else was there?'

'What about Jay Langerud?'

Suspicion tickled her neck. She'd experienced guilt often enough to know the signs. She tried to sound genuinely bemused. 'What about him?'

'He was fast today. I was fast. I thought I put him

behind me, but when the chips were down, he was as easy to wear as a handmade suit.'

'What are you saying, that you like being a gunfighter?'

'No. I never liked it, wondering whether I was faster than the next man. But what if that's the man I really am?' He looked her in the eye, the glint of mischief she was accustomed to seeing, strangely absent. 'You've been through enough, Ros, you and your family. I can't ask to marry a killer.'

She came to her knees. 'You're not a killer. You fought because you had to. What else could you have done except stand there and let Radley shoot holes through you? This is not you. You embrace life. I'm the one who's afraid of it, afraid of the past, afraid of the future. What's happened?'

His eyes narrowed and it was a minute before he answered her. 'Jimmy says he wants to be just like me. Bang, bang, bang. He wants me to teach him the quick draw.'

Ros breathed a sigh of relief. 'What's wrong with that?'

'I started out like Jimmy. The first man I ever killed was the man who killed my pa.'

'And you became a marshal. Now you're a sheriff. What's wrong with that?'

'I told you, I was lucky. I could just as easily have gone on the way I was – killing.'

She didn't believe it, despite what she'd seen out in the street, but the way Jake was acting it would take a miracle to change his mind. And maybe she had one. . . .

'If the boy's worrying you that much, why don't you share some of your luck with him?'

'Share my luck?' he asked, confusion finally rousing him from his daze-like despondency.

'You talked about wanting a family, having what Matt and Ava have. Why not you, me and Jimmy?'

He stared at her, the mood visibly lifting from him like a veil.

'I'm serious, Jake. You can teach him to use a gun, for the right reasons.'

His teeth flashed in the lamplight. 'You're going to make a great wife.'